An Oven Beyond

Laughing Loaf Bakery Mystery #6

Victoria Kazarian

For Armen and Lisa

So excited that you're off in your own spaces,
writing as I write.
May it bring you as much joy as it's brought me.

Chapter One

It seemed unreal.

To my assistant, Beck Rodriguez, it was like saying goodbye to a beloved coworker.

We watched solemnly as her husband, Sam, and my boyfriend, Nate, tipped our aqua, 1950s-era refrigerator back onto the dolly that would carry it out to Sam's pickup truck.

The small fridge—which Beck called The Little Fridge that Could—would be replaced by a large aluminum industrial fridge. We'd need a bigger second fridge, since we were preparing to start lunch service at The Laughing Loaf Bakery in July. We'd need more room for condiments, supplies, and cold proofing the loaves for sandwich bread.

I'd inherited the aqua fridge from the burger joint that had occupied our 1920s brick bank building on River Grove's main street. The old Philco refrigerator was adorably midcentury and had turned out to be more reliable than our modern refurbished industrial fridge.

Saying goodbye to it meant we were really going

through with this renovation. But we had lots to do before then. A lot of dust, a lot of inconvenience.

Beck, who only liked change when it happened to our menu, blinked back tears as she watched Sam and Nate head toward the front door with the appliance.

"It'll be so different not having it here." Beck brushed her eyes with the back of her hand.

Maeve Killoran, who joined us as a baker in December, was not nearly as sentimental as Beck.

"Beck, remember. The Little Fridge that Could is going to *your house*. You'll get to use it every day," she said in her Irish brogue. With a mischievous smile, she went over to the music system above the baking table, and clicked a song on her music app. Soon Sarah MacLachlan's "I Will Remember You" played throughout the back room.

As the mournful, soft rock ballad played through the back room's speakers, we went to the front window and watched the fridge as it rolled toward the truck, Nate's and Sam's hands steadying it. Then the two men lifted it up onto the lowered tailgate and pushed it onto the truck bed.

With the sad song playing, I felt like we needed a commemorative video montage, showing the times that little fridge had saved the day—the times we'd jammed it with all of our butter and milk when the motor in our big fridge died. Or the time, before we installed air conditioning, when we'd stocked it with Beck's lemonade and homemade popsicles to cool ourselves off when the temps in the back room were in the 90s.

"The new refrigerator will be delivered tomorrow between 11:30 and 1:30." I grabbed the broom and began sweeping the spot vacated by the aqua appliance. "On Monday let's look at the plan we came up with for reorganizing the back room. Demolition and construction on the front counter and dining area start in two weeks. The back room will stay open so we can bake and prep, but we won't have a front counter for a while. We might be able to keep the bakery open for limited hours—they're working on a plan for us to stay open till 11:30 a.m."

The phone in my pocket buzzed. I pulled it out. It was Redwood Commercial Renovations.

"Hi, is this Gracie Markley? Helen Fields, Redwood's scheduler. We've been trying to accommodate your request for a later work schedule so you can keep your business open for the morning. Hank, our owner, wanted me to make sure you understand the cost increase."

She told me the full price, which was almost double the original estimate. And the date of completion would be pushed out a month.

I'd been hoping to keep my bakery open for at least part of the day during renovation. I knew it would be crazy and messy, but I didn't want to have to close The Laughing Loaf.

"Wait a minute." I rubbed my forehead. "Jeff, the man who went over the costs, didn't tell me it would be this expensive."

The scheduler heaved a long sigh.

"Jeff is no longer an estimator with Redwood Commercial Renovations. He had a habit of making promises we couldn't keep."

I watched my plans for the next month circle the drain.

"What? We can't afford that cost increase."

She continued tersely. "I apologize that you were misinformed, Ms. Markley. We can complete the job for you—and you can keep your business open for part of the day—but it will be at the higher cost."

There was no going away to think about this. I'd wanted

to keep The Laughing Loaf open. But I couldn't justify or even afford the cost. I couldn't delay completion; I wanted the renovated bakery to open before students went back to school in August.

"Fine." My jaw clenched. "We'll keep to the original schedule. We will figure out some way to work with the situation."

Blissfully unaware of my conversation with our contractor, Beck went back to fill apple tarts on the metal table. "I can't wait till we start serving lunch. I've been testing dessert recipes at home."

Beck, our resident Queen of Pastry, had been taking classes on new techniques. I was looking forward to seeing what she'd come up with for dessert—and I was eager to taste the results.

"I've got some sourdough variations I'd like to try, for sandwich bread," Maeve said. Until last December, Maeve had worked at the critically acclaimed Night Rose bakery in Sonoma, where she manned the register but didn't bake. "Rafal gave me some ideas. I was thinking of working on them at Mayor C's while I'm here during the week."

Maeve's friend, Rafal, had tutored her in bread-baking after hours, and she worked as an assistant breadmaker on weekends with him at his new place of employment, a bakery called Pain Parisienne, in Napa's wine country. On weekdays, she rented a room at the house of River Grove town mayor and softball coach, Corinne Webster.

"Maeve, you're more than welcome to do test bakes here," I said. "You have a key."

"That's what I do," Beck piped up as she laid apple slices in precise spirals in the tart pans. "I stay late and bake here. I play music and experiment with recipes I've been wanting to try. You should join me."

My assistant manager and my apprentice bread baker immediately started planning a baking night. The two of them, close in age but with very different personalities and backgrounds, were forming a friendship. Beck was sweetly naive and traditional, while Maeve, who'd grown up in urban Dublin, Ireland, was cynical and sharp-witted. Now the two of them pulled up stools and leaned over the table laughing and sharing their baking ideas. Their delight was infectious, and I began to feel less stressed about the hitch in our renovation plans.

I headed to the front of the bakery to do a final wipe-down of the tables.

With the start of daylight savings time, the sky outside was still cornflower blue at 5 p.m., and the sun shone through the big windows in the Laughing Loaf's empty dining room.

Two months ago, Beck, Maeve, and I sat down with the initial plan we'd gotten from the contractor. We tried to picture how the natural flow of employees and customers would work. Customers should know where to put in their order and where to pick it up. Employees needed to have a convenient fridge for milks, a sink, and a prep counter. The path between these things had to be quick and well thought out. We'd have more employees in the space and they needed to get to what they needed without running into each other.

I stood at the door, looking in, and tried to picture what everything would look like in two months, based on the designer's plans—the round counter in front, and the reddish gleam of the new chairs and tables I'd picked out, which would give the bakery a streamlined modern look, while also paying homage to River Grove's redwood logging past.

Thankfully, the county had approved our permit last week without a hitch.

Now, if we could only get through the process without more delays. The Laughing Loaf was in a hundred-year-old building. I hoped the contractors didn't uncover hidden problems in the aging structure.

Nate had returned from the Rodriguez house and was getting out of his car in front of the bakery. Tonight, he had softball practice, under the watchful eye of the team's coach, Mayor C. This Friday was the season opener for the River Grove River Rats softball team.

I met him at the door. He leaned in toward me, one hand on the doorframe, and gave me a kiss that made my legs wobbly.

He had that shy look on his face that I loved: he was trying not to smile, but his mouth fought him and won, turning up at the corners.

"The fridge is hooked up and working in Sam and Beck's kitchen. I'm on my way home before I head over to Grove Park for practice. Wanna get together afterwards for some dinner?"

"Of course." Still feeling lightheaded from the kiss, and annoyed by the call from the contractor, I relaxed against his chest. Between a nature photo shoot on the Sacramento River and his practices for the River Grove River Rats soft-ball team, I hadn't seen much of Nate this week.

He looked around the bakery, curious. "So, when does the work start?"

"In two weeks." I lost excitement even as I said the words. "From what the contractors are saying now, we'll have to close the bakery for at least two weeks. I thought we could keep it open during construction—even if it was only mornings. Turns out it's almost double the cost."

Nate thought for a moment, his light blue eyes catching a glint from the sun.

"What if you took the bakery somewhere else for those two weeks? Have you ever been to a pop-up? LA has pop-up restaurants and shops all the time. People want to visit them more because they're temporary and a unique experience. They don't want to miss out."

"I've been to one in the Pacific Northwest." I remembered visiting a pop-up cafe in Seattle. "I can't think of a place in River Grove where we could do one."

The idea intrigued me; even during the remodel of the front counter and dining area, we'd still be able to use the back room for baking and staging. All we needed was a place to sell our baked goods and connect with customers.

"You can have it wherever you can find a space, Gracie."

"Yeah, but I don't have a lot of time to figure it out." I'd need to move on this soon. I wanted to brainstorm with my employees. But I needed to do some brainstorming with myself first.

"You should get to practice." I straightened up as I heard Beck and Maeve preparing to head out to dinner. "Don't let Mayor C boss you around."

"She always does." He laughed. "The opener with the Gilroy team is supposed to be an easy win, but you never know. Mayor C's been drilling us all week at practices. She's not putting the same pressure on us as she was before. So hopefully no injuries—"

"Like during that first practice." I groaned, and Nate turned bright red, not wanting a reminder of the painful groin pull he received catching a fly ball six weeks ago.

"Yeah, my goal is to avoid doing that again. I'll give you a call when we're done." He planted a kiss on my forehead.

"Dad'll be out at tutoring sessions." My father, Dr. John Markley, a retired physics professor, had recently started tutoring Advanced Placement Physics students from River Grove High School. I could see it in the way he carried himself, the glow on his face. Tutoring was bringing him new life. He was doing what he loved again.

Two years ago, witness protection relocated my father, me and my little dog Biga from Seattle to the small town of River Grove in the California redwoods. After I found records of foreign transactions on his computer, I put the pieces together and turned in my ex-husband Ben for selling tech secrets. After that, my life changed completely; in retrospect, it was for the better. I traded my job in the tech industry to do something I'd always loved—bake bread. And I traded my marriage to a self-obsessed narcissist for a relationship with a gentle, 6'4" boy scout of a man who made his living photographing birds.

"It'll be nice to have some time together before things get crazy for both of us." Nate gave me one of those shy, yearning looks that made me melt. "Once the season starts and I head out of town on my shoots, it'll be tough to find the time."

I WENT to my dog Biga's pen, just off the back room of the bakery. He looked up at me suspiciously. The FOMO was strong with my dog. He was sure something was going on and he wasn't invited. I set his crate into the pen and coaxed him into it.

"Biga boy, your buddy Nate is coming over tonight. But

you'll be staying home on Friday. You'd just wait for kids to drop their hot dogs." I shut the grate on his travel crate and went to my office to grab my purse. Beck and Maeve were still at the metal table talking excitedly, letting out occasional hoots of laughter. Maeve was helping Beck fill another pan of tarts.

"I'm taking off now, you two." I put my bag over my shoulder and grabbed the bin with aprons to be washed.

"We're going to get breadsticks at RG's Pizza," Beck said excitedly. "We might come back and do a late-night baking session."

"Sounds like a lot of fun." I smiled, thinking Beck must *really* want to hang out with Maeve since she was not a fan of RG's. "Remember to take the trash out to the dumpster when you leave."

"We will, Gracie," Beck called while taking off her apron. "Oh, and Sam says he wants to see Nate's game on Friday."

Nate was a natural athlete. And, as I tried to tell Mayor C when she was recruiting for the River Grove softball team, I definitely was *not*.

My ex-husband Ben hadn't been either, unless you count juggling secret overseas bank accounts and hiding them from your wife as an athletic activity.

After I found out that Ben had been selling defense secrets to Russia, China and North Korea, I turned him in to the FBI—after he threatened to say I was in on the scheme with him.

It was scary sitting down in front of an agent and telling him what I'd found on Ben's computer. It was even scarier when I testified against Ben in court, and I looked out to see him giving me a murderous glare.

When I'd turned Ben in, it had shut down the pipeline

of secrets. There were foreign governments who were not happy with me--and some who were sure I took some of Ben's secrets with me. I'd had a run-in with some Russian agents last year. And while that had ended well for me, I couldn't be sure it wouldn't happen again.

"We need to get a group together for Friday night," I suggested. "Stake out a Nate Behrens cheering section in the bleachers."

"Sam and I will be there. We'll bring treats!" Beck called out from the back, where she was tying up a trash bag.

Maeve waved as she slung her purse over her shoulder. She'd be heading back to Napa on Friday night to her weekend job.

"I'm sad I can't join you all. Go, River Rats!"

WHEN I CAME through my front door of our house, my father was in the kitchen in his professorial corduroy blazer and slacks, preparing himself a chicken salad sandwich with the focus of a scientist conducting an experiment.

He used a knife to sweep piles of precisely chopped apples and walnuts from the cutting board into the mixing bowl of chicken. Then he scooped mayonnaise from a jar into a measuring cup and smoothed a knife across it, then held it up to his eyes to see that it was perfectly level.

Last year, I'd started teaching him how to make food for himself, and he'd come a long way since then. His on-again-off-again girlfriend Mary Jo Hartman had continued teaching him in the kitchen, as they made dinner together.

"A quick dinner before I take off to tutor tonight. My students are in a panic about next month's AP test, so I've started a series of group review sessions."

"Poor kids." I thought about the high school juniors and seniors he was tutoring, many of whom I saw in the bakery before school. "Tell them good luck for me."

I took Biga out in the back yard and chased him around for a few minutes so he got his exercise. After a squirrel appeared on the back fence, he lost all interest in me. Despite being brought up on Beatrix Potter books, I am not a fan of squirrels, and neither was Biga. He chased the furry fiend back and forth indignantly until it leaped for dear life onto a tree on the other side of the fence.

Good riddance.

I called my boy inside and filled his water and food bowls. Then I set up gates to keep him from places in the house where I knew he'd get into trouble. Places where he had a track record: the kitchen and my dad's study. He'd once stashed his slobbery chew toys in my dad's slippers. Not a pleasant experience slipping them on in the morning.

As Biga dug into his dinner, I opened the fridge. I had a large container of butter chicken, which I could heat up for Nate and me. If we were going to have leftovers, we might as well have really good leftovers. I'd steam some vegetables, make basmati rice, and open a bottle of pinot. We were set.

Nate wouldn't be here till 6:30 p.m., so in the meantime, I stretched out on the sofa and drafted a smaller, more manageable menu for our pop-up—the location of which I didn't even know yet. I kept most of the crowd pleasers: cinnamon rolls, tarts, scones and some of our breads. Beck's beignets and anything else fried would be off the menu for that time, since they were best served fresh and wouldn't hold up for long.

After I'd gotten up and prepared our meal, I heard a familiar knock on the door. Biga skittered to the front hallway, barking furiously.

As soon as I opened the door, Biga put his paws up on Nate's legs, licking his hands. Nate squatted down and cuddled the guy.

"Two minutes ago, he thought you were an axe murderer," I said, rolling my eyes.

"He was just being cautious. I *could* have been an axe murderer." Nate stood up, a white bag in his hand, which immediately got my attention. White bags and pink boxes are a definite tipoff of delicious treats inside. "What kind of a watchdog would he be if he let me in? He couldn't live with that on his conscience."

When we went into the dining room, he casually set the bag on the table without a word.

I was curious and so was Biga, who looked up and sniffed as he circled the table.

"So...what's in the bag?"

"Our pitcher, Ted Daigle—his wife made blueberry hand pies, so he brought some to practice. They're good. I asked if I could take some with me. He told me, 'Only if Gracie gets one.'"

I laughed. "He really said that? Then I've got to have one. How was practice?"

My boyfriend frowned as he took a seat at the dining room table and stretched his long legs out. I poured us each a glass of wine. Nate immediately took a big gulp.

"Practice didn't get started till almost 5:30. Councilman Gregg was late and in a bad mood when he showed up. He was snapping at everyone. He almost got in a fistfight with Marla Sorenson if you can believe that. The two were going at it, hissing like a couple of birds circling to attack. Corinne got between them, and then things cooled down."

I set the butter chicken and rice on the table and took a seat. "Do you know what it was about?"

Nate shook his head and started loading up his plate. "No clue. They kept their voices low. Whatever it was, he must have put all that frustration into his hitting. He knocked it out of the park twice during batting practice."

"I hope he does that Friday."

Nate smiled. "Mayor C's counting on it."

"You have an entourage for the opener so far. Beck, Sam, Elana, Kirk, Chloe, and the chief are joining me in the bleachers to cheer you on."

Nate laughed, a little embarrassed. "What about your dad?"

I raised my eyebrows and smiled. "He's a Brit. He says baseball's got nothing on cricket."

"Fair enough." Nate smiled. He continued till he quickly finished off his butter chicken and rice. "Gracie, I can't believe this was leftovers."

I finally broke into the mysterious white bag and served our hand pies on plates, topped with a scoop of vanilla ice cream. The dark, sweet blueberry filling was delicious as it melded with the ice cream.

"What's Ted's wife's name? Paula? I've seen her come into the bakery a few times. If I don't see her, please tell Ted thanks. These are so good."

"I'll pass that on."

We talked about what a pop-up might look like. I shared my proposed pop-up menu with Nate.

I should be excited about this renovation. This was a huge step forward for The Laughing Loaf. We'd be providing a lunch option, which wasn't available in River Grove. But as I'd talked to customers in River Grove who'd done renovations, both at home and at their businesses, I'd heard horror stories of delays and cost overruns, when structural issues were discovered in their old buildings.

"Our house in LA had faulty wiring and an earthquake-damaged chimney. It was a California bungalow, built in 1926. And the repairs dragged out the project." Nate shook his head. "Nico's modeling income took care of most of it, but it was expensive." Nate's younger brother Nico had been killed outside the Laughing Loaf. For three years before that, he'd been a successful model in LA, until he'd been accused of a jewel theft.

I frowned and slunk down in my chair. This was not news I wanted to hear. I wanted my shiny new counter and dining area done and open for business as quickly and painlessly as possible.

The pop-up could be fun, but it was a little like the retail equivalent of camping. I wanted to get back in our regular space and had no desire to work in a tent for weeks.

Nate saw the look on my face and his eyes turned sympathetic. "You don't know any of this is going to happen yet, Gracie. There may be delays. If there are, I know you'll deal with them just fine."

I sat up and scraped the last bits of blueberry filling from my plate with a fork. "I guess if we have to be in the pop-up a little longer, it won't be the worst thing."

And it wouldn't be.

If only because so many other bad things *were* going to happen.

Things that I couldn't even imagine right now.

Chapter Two

Before opening the bakery the next morning, I set the joke of the day on its stand. Some of my favorite jokes of the day were ones people had to think about for a few seconds.

Laughing Loaf Joke of the Day
You don't need a parachute to go skydiving.
You need one to go skydiving twice.

It was the team's rest day before the season opener, and it went by quickly. The high schoolers came and went, with their usual energy and high noise level.

Shortly afterwards, River Grove Police Chief Dave Westerman and Mayor Corinne Webster—Beck and I had given them the celebrity couple name, *Websterman*—came in for their usual meeting at the corner table.

Usually they conducted themselves seriously, as they discussed current crime and public safety issues in River Grove.

Today the two of them drank their coffee and conversed

casually about what colleges the chief's granddaughter, Chloe, was planning to visit this fall, and then details of River Rats season opening softball game.

At 9 a.m., another visitor from City Hall across the street, Councilman Keith Gregg, came up to the front counter. He was a long, wiry man with an almost permanent scowl and a rapidly receding hairline. He seemed slightly hunched over—almost if he were preparing to catch a hit in the outfield during a softball game. I'd heard of him more than seen him around River Grove. His batting, as Nate had told me, was supposed to be legendary.

Mayor C said he usually got his coffee from the gas station on the way into town—which seemed like a sad life to me.

"Good morning, Councilman. What can I get you today?"

"Gimme a medium latte with whole milk and a couple of those scones." He fished in his back pocket for his wallet. He pulled a five dollar bill out of it and laid it on the counter. I looked up at him, puzzled.

"Councilman, your total with tax is 7.29."

"That's ridiculous." A look of contempt twisted his features. "I don't know where you're from, but you have no right charging those big city prices here in River Grove."

"I'm sorry, Councilman, but that's the price. It's in line with what people are charging everywhere."

I was definitely not as sweet as my assistant, Beck, but I do try to give angry customers the benefit of the doubt. Everyone can have an off day.

"What if you just got the coffee?" I put on a friendly smile. "That would bring you down to about five dollars."

"Fine. I'll be damned if I'll come here again. The gas station was out when I stopped by." He waited for Beck to set his latte down on the counter. Then he took it with a frown, turned on his heels and left through the front door.

I looked over at the mayor and the chief at the corner table, but neither of them had heard our exchange.

I didn't have time to stew about his testy response because it was a busy day.

We had several orders to fill for company get-togethers this week, including one for the Santa Cruz software company, Bluesoft, run by my best friend Elana's husband.

Mayor C had also ordered two dozen cupcakes with rats and baseball bats on them, like the ones we'd made for the River Rats' first practice.

Beck, Maeve and I stayed late to mold the rats and baseball bats out of fondant then frost the cupcakes and decorate them.

Softball was River Grove's most widely attended sport, aside from kids' soccer and Little League. The River Rats had been playing in the Mountain Coastal Intramural League since the 1970s. It was another town tradition that brought everyone together.

River Grovians could get fiercely competitive, whether the occasion was a chili cookoff or an athletic competition.

Us-against-them was a powerful unifier in our small town, and tomorrow night that town spirit would be focused like a laser on the Gilroy Garlic Heads. I was nervous about that but excited to be part of it at the same time.

"Why don't you and Sam meet here tomorrow evening and we can walk over to Grove Park?" I picked up a tray of finished cupcakes and slid them into our sleek new industrial refrigerator.

Beck looked up from the fondant rat she was making finishing touches to. The adorable, smiling rodent looked way cuter than its real-life counterparts.

"That sounds good, Gracie. Oh, and can my brothers Eric and Korben sit with us, too? They're coming to the game, and they want to hang out with us."

Beck had five older brothers. From Beck's descriptions of her family, Eric and Korben were the youngest boys, two and three years older than Beck. Apart from Beck's stories of them teasing their little sister, they didn't seem too objectionable.

"Sure, Beck. Let's all meet here at 5:30. I want to make sure we've got enough space in the bleachers. Mayor C says the season opener gets crazy crowded."

Our group was growing, nine of us so far with the chief and Chloe. With this many people, I just hoped everyone would get along.

"I'm bringing lemonade in a carrier," Beck said. "And some popcorn. Do you think we need anything else? Chloe told me she's bringing brownies."

"Then we're set. I'm bringing a charcuterie board. I'll load on more meat and cheese. We should be good."

When I came home from the bakery the next evening, after the usual busy Friday, my father was in his study, typing up a tutoring handout on his computer.

I poked my head in the doorway.

"Biga's feeling left out, since he's not going tonight—"

My father swiveled toward me in his chair. "Don't worry, dear. Biga and I are spending the evening together. He won't be missing anything."

My father issued this statement with such confidence, I snorted in laughter. "What exciting slate of activities do you have planned, Dad?"

I thought of Mary Jo, his girlfriend-on-hold, whom I'd resented at first but had started to like. Since they decided to take a break from each other, I'd started to miss her. "No lady friend tonight?"

He shook his head. "Mary Jo and I spoke yesterday and are planning to get together next week. We've been talking quite a bit on the phone." As usual, the Physics presentation on his screen was pulling his attention away like a magnet. He inched closer to the screen, probably hoping I'd go away and leave him alone.

Not a chance.

"So, by *talking*, Dad, you mean you are telling her how you feel and asking what she's thinking and feeling? And you're talking about things that aren't physics principles or food. Like what you both want and need from your relationship." My father carefully avoided anything with emotion or complications attached.

He visibly shuddered. "Really, Gracie, I—"

I went over and gave him a hug. "I'm not trying to give you a hard time. It's just that I know for a fact you care about Mary Jo, and I know she cares about you. Tell her when you need time to yourself. When you don't communicate with her, she thinks you're not interested. This isn't just my opinion—she actually told me that."

"It's difficult to talk about these things." My father shook his head.

"Physics is difficult," I said with an affectionate smile. "Telling people how you feel isn't that hard."

After my little TED Talk, I filled Biga's water and food bowls.

While Biga dove into his dinner, I wrapped up the charcuterie board and sourdough I was bringing to tonight's gathering.

I paused in the doorway to my room, as I considered what to wear to a softball game—a softball game where I'd be drinking really good wine.

I rooted through my drawers. And admittedly, I pawed through the clean laundry pile on my chair that hadn't yet made it into my drawers. I pulled out an olive-green fitted t-shirt and shook the wrinkles out. I chose a thick coffee-colored hoodie, and some warm leggings, which I'd wear with ankle boots.

As soon as the sun went down, Grove Park would get chilly. I'm not sure my friend, Elana, was thinking of that. She was very interested in fashion and a lot less interested in practicality.

AFTER I PARKED my Subaru in the alley behind the Laughing Loaf, I got out to see Beck, her brothers, and Sam heading up the steps into the bakery. I took out my small cooler and slipped its strap over my shoulder.

"Gracie!" Beck hugged me excitedly when I stepped up into the back room, even though she'd just seen me at the bakery an hour ago, but then that was Beck. "I can't remember if you've met Eric. And Korben."

Eric leaned against the metal table, his arms crossed tightly across his chest. "Uh, hi, Gracie." He was long and bony. His eyes darted nervously around the group of us.

Korben, a stocky young man with an infectious grin, came up to me, grabbed my hands with both of his and shook them heartily. His dark brown eyes lit up with sheer joy. "Gracie! Thanks for letting us sit with you tonight. We brought chips and salsa. So excited to see Nate on the team tonight. Sam says he's an amazing player."

Korben was, basically, the male equivalent of his friendly and effusive sister.

There was a knock at the back door and I saw the chief peer through the glass, with his granddaughter, Chloe, behind him.

I opened the door and the two of them joined us. The chief seemed in a good mood. Chloe and Beck immediately hugged and started laughing and whispering about something.

I wouldn't call myself a raging extrovert, but I love getting groups of people together to socialize and have fun. It's why I'm so glad The Laughing Loaf had become a popular meeting place in River Grove. When people connect with each other, I'm in my happy place. And tonight, I was prepared to have that same happy feeling.

Unfortunately, tonight would not be that kind of an event.

Everyone gathered their treats, jackets, and blankets, and we set out for Grove Park, chatting, laughing and exchanging stories as we crossed the street. We walked past The Riverside Saloon, then continued toward the park where we'd meet up with Elana and Kirk and stake out our space on the bleachers. The sun had slipped down behind the trees. There was some light, but it was fading fast.

When I realized Eric and Korben were walking behind me, I turned around and smiled.

"You probably came to these games when you were kids, right?"

Korben nodded. "Oh, sure. Dad took us boys. Beck came sometimes, too, but Mom wasn't into it. My dad bought us hot dogs and we got to see friends we only saw at homeschool meetups. There's not much going on in River Grove, so this was big entertainment."

Eric spoke up. "The River Rats didn't win very often. It was pathetic. We came out to cheer, then it was a big letdown for us kids."

"Wait a minute—" I wanted to get this straight. As a relative newcomer, I had a lot of River Grove history to catch up on. "They didn't win back then?"

Korben laughed. "Mayor C is way better than the River Rats coaches in the past. She actually wins games."

I heard the chief behind me. "Been true since I've been here. Corinne's actually gotten the team into the finals. We're lucky to have her."

THE RIVER RATS home field stood at the far corner of Grove Park, and as we approached, fans were slowly streaming up into the grey, weathered wooden bleachers.

Since the lower levels were filling up, I called to our party that we needed to head up to the higher seats. I scanned the crowd for Elana and Kirk.

Then I saw them waving near the top. Even from here, I could tell Elana had brought all the fancy accoutrements. She was holding up a wine glass.

"Hey, girl!" I heard Elana's voice call out while we were still a few benches down. I couldn't miss my friend. She was practically glowing radioactively in a bright white jeans jacket, enormous sunglasses and a rhinestone-studded baseball cap. She and Kirk had spread blankets across the benches to save room for our group and soften the effect of the hard, unforgiving bench.

When I reached her, She hugged me. "We saved a *lot* of seats. It fills up so fast."

I sat down next to Elana, as the rest of our party settled in place down the bench.

"I haven't been to a game in years," she said, popping an olive into her mouth. "I think the last time was that season you played, Kirk."

"A season I want to forget," Kirk stood up to greet me. "Good to see you, Gracie."

I gave him a hug. The past three months had been tough on Kirk, as he dealt with the software release from hell and the death of his lead programmer.

"Are things getting better at BlueSoft?" I asked.

Kirk was clean shaven and less gaunt than when I'd seen him last.

"We're getting there." He nodded slowly. "I can take a break tonight and know everything's not going to fall to pieces."

We were three rows from the top in the stands, directly above the River Rat dugout, and had a good view of the field. A cool wind blew through the bleachers, and I wondered if by the time the sun dipped behind the trees, we might be wearing the blankets we were sitting on, to keep warm.

I set down the insulated carrier bag between Elana and me.

"I brought a charcuterie board and some sourdough bread. Down the bench, we've got popcorn, Beck's lemonade, and Chloe Westerman's brownies."

Elana always brightened at the prospect of food. "Charcuterie! That'll be perfect with the tempranillo I brought." She gave me a serious look. "Please tell me it's got cheese."

"You know me, Elana." I pretended to be offended. "Do you really think *I'd* forget the cheese?"

Elana sighed with relief and pulled a bottle out of her bag. "This wine *requires* cheese."

Kirk produced a corkscrew-type implement he kept on

his keychain and within a minute had the bottle open. Elana poured deep red wine into plastic wine glasses for us. We raised them.

Kirk tapped his plastic wine glass against mine and Elana's. "To Nate's new career as a first baseman."

The River Rats were warming up out in the field—which, unlike a baseball field, was smaller and not grassy—just dirt. Nate stood near first base, throwing the bright yellow ball easily back and forth with the other basemen.

I love to watch people who are good at something I have no skill in.

Nate had this way of catching with only the smallest of movements; he locked onto the ball approaching and barely moved his glove to catch it. I watched with fascination, it looked so effortless. Another reason Mayor C should be thankful that it was him on the team and not me.

While we nibbled at the charcuterie and drank our wine, River Grovians settled in around us in the bleachers.

The chief, who sat a few feet down from us on the bench, saw my wine glass and charcuterie board and shot me a look of disdain.

"Wine at a softball game, Markley? C'mon."

Eric and Korben had gone down to the concessions stand, and a few minutes later came back with boxes of hot dogs and chips. The aroma of the hot dogs topped with Day-Glo yellow mustard brought back memories of going to Mariners games in Seattle. I might, for just a minute or two, have regretted tonight's gourmet food choices.

I scanned the field below. The River Rats streamed in from the field and headed for the dugout.

I saw a player who looked out of place in the group. Someone familiar, but the last person I'd expect to see on a softball field. I leaned forward in my seat, wine glass in hand.

"Hey! Wait a minute."

Between second and third base stood a short young woman. It could only be Peony Roberts, city hall's receptionist and, occasionally, my personal nemesis. "She's in uniform. It's got to be her."

Elana almost spit out her wine. Kirk pulled out a pair of binoculars and looked down at the field.

"Yep, that's her." He focused in on the field. "Looks like she's shortstop."

Mayor C was relentless when recruiting for the River Rats. In her quest for team members, she worked her way through downtown businesses with the heavy-handedness of a mobster demanding protection money.

Why hadn't Nate mentioned Peony was on the team?

I wondered how much pressure Mayor C had applied to get her to join the team. I mean, was Peony here against her will?

Nate had told me that according to the rules of the league, the River Rats had to have a quota of women on the team. Peony worked a few feet away from Mayor C. That could be why she was here: it was an arrangement of convenience.

The team had settled into the dugout. Mayor C walked back and forth in front of them, but I couldn't hear what she was saying. Probably a pre-game pep talk. Or knowing the mayor, threats.

As she talked, a five-foot tall, grey furry creature with a bedraggled tail walked out to the infield and began holding his arms up in the air. Then he put his hands to his lips and blew kisses to the stands. The crowd around me exploded in cheers.

I had a feeling I was in for yet another quirky River Grove tradition.

The chant began. All the members of our group joined in enthusiastically—The chief, Chloe, Sam and Beck, and her brothers.

"Runty! Runty! Runty! Runty!"

Soon feet were stomping, and hands were clapping along with the chant. The bleachers shook beneath us.

What the heck.

I shot a look at Elana and Kirk, who were laughing as if this was the funniest thing they'd ever seen. They started clapping.

The rat did a little jig, then ran to the other side of the bleachers to start them in the chant. Soon everyone on the bleachers—except, well, *me*—was stomping, clapping and chanting. I finally joined in.

After the creature did one last shuffle across the sidelines of the diamond, the crowd erupted into a cheer.

"River Rats, River Rats, RI-VER RAAAATS!"

Runty grabbed his long tail and waved it saucily at the crowd, as the sound guy played a snippet of strip-tease music.

Then Runty made his exit, making a beeline for the concession stand at the back of the bleachers.

"So that was—" I turned to Elana and Kirk.

"Runty. Runty the River Rat," Elana said matter of factly. "He's always the star of the show. He gets the crowd going before every game. Kai Daniels played Runty for a few years. You have to be small enough to fit the suit. I don't know who does it now. Do you, Kirk?"

Kirk took a sip of his wine and raised his eyebrows. "No idea."

The loudspeaker started up with a squawk of feedback.

"Welcome all to the first game of the Mountain-Coastal Intramural League softball season here at Grove Park Field. Tonight, River Grove and The River Rats host the Garlic Heads from Gilroy."

The crowd cheered. I assumed the small crowd on the bleachers along the first base line was filled with Gilroy fans, since they only came to life when their team's name was called. A few of them wore goofy, garlic bulb hats on their heads.

"Please rise for the singing of our national anthem. Singing for us tonight is River Grove High School's own Amelia Kate Gruber."

Chloe Westerman stood up and cheered her friend. When I saw her stand up, I did, too.

Amelia, who did her homework in the bakery most weekdays before school with her friends, held a microphone as she stood stiffly in front of the dugout. She looked pale and terrified. With no accompaniment, she began singing into the mic, her voice wavering at first. Once she got going, though, she seemed to visibly relax. By the time she reached the end of the song, she belted out the final *of the brave* confidently. Both sides of the bleachers erupted in applause.

THE CEREMONIAL PITCH, in this first game of the season, was thrown out by Scotty Baxter, 1986 River Grove Chili Cookoff winner. It made sense. He was, for reasons I wasn't sure I completely understood, the closest thing River Grove had to a celebrity. Grinning and waving to the crowd, the grizzled 75-year-old Scotty walked out to the mound and threw a decent underhand pitch roughly in the direction of home plate.

Sam, Beck and her brothers stood up and cheered, along with most people in the River Grove bleachers.

The River Rats were up to bat first.

A woman with curly, white-blonde hair peeking out from under her helmet stood at the plate. Two pitches that were clearly strikes whizzed past her, then she hit a foul ball that landed on the sidelines. On the next pitch, unfortunately, she hit a ground ball directly toward first base. The first baseman calmly scooped it up, and she was out before she made it to base.

Elana leaned toward me. "That's Marla Sorenson. She manages Spinnetti's Sparkletown Cleaners. Rumor has it she's Mayor C's ex-girlfriend. They're just friends now. She's usually a great hitter."

"I'm surprised I haven't met her yet," I said, reaching for another roll of prosciutto from the charcuterie. I wondered how Elana knew all these things. Then I remembered when the whole town seemed to know Nate and I were dating— before we even did.

I shook my head as the woman walked back to the dugout. "She had really bad luck on that hit, though."

Elana downed a gulp of tempranillo. "No kidding. That was just embarrassing."

Nate stepped into the warmup spot and to practice his swing.

Next up to bat was Peony Roberts. She strode up to the plate, a long braid swinging from the back of her baseball cap. She settled into an impressively legit batter's stance. When the first ball whizzed past her, Peony didn't move an inch. The umpire called a strike.

She glared at the pitcher with the kind of look she regularly gave me when denying me access to the city hall back offices.

The pitch came, and with a resounding *thwack* the ball headed for the outfield. Peony ran toward first base while a Gilroy player in centerfield bobbled and dropped the ball. By the time he threw it to the baseman, Peony had a foot firmly on base.

The hometown crowd was on its feet, cheering.

"Damn!" Elana turned to me in awe. "That girl can play ball. How come I didn't know this?"

When Nate walked up to the plate, my stomach sputtered with anxiety. I wanted him to do well. He could catch, obviously, but I'd never seen him play. Could he hit?

Our entourage on the bench began cheering for Nate.

The first pitch was low and inside. The second pitch came fast and Nate swung—and missed. I could see him look down and take a deep breath. He held up the bat and waited. When the pitch came, he hit a powerful grounder between second and third base. The field exploded in a flurry of action. Peony headed for second, and Nate landed quickly on first. Both runners were safe.

Councilman Gregg approached the plate.

"Nate says this guy is their star hitter," I told Elana and Kirk. I felt a shiver of excitement. If he hit it out of the park, as he'd done on at Wednesday practice, Peony and Nate would score runs.

"Bring it on, Councilman!" Elana yelled, addressing the man himself. "Let's get this party started!"

Maybe the pitcher was intimidated. Maybe his plan was to walk the councilman to keep him from hitting it past the fence, which he was known for.

The first two pitches looked too high even to my untrained eye, and the umpire called them as balls. The third pitch looked way outside the zone. When the fourth pitch was the same, the councilman walked to first, Nate walked calmly to second, and Peony headed for third.

Bases were loaded. I was no softball expert, but I knew this was a good setup for the River Rats—as long as whoever was batting next hit it out of the park.

"Oh my God. This is *too* exciting," Elana took a sip of her wine. She shivered and pulled her stylish but thin jacket tightly around her. "Now who's up next?"

Kirk leaned forward and looked down as a man approached the plate. "Looks like Jake Daniels. Didn't know he was on the team this year. He played when I did, three years ago."

Elana and I were invested in this now. We both looked at him, and started in at the same time: "But is he any *good?*"

Kirk looked amused. "So you two fancy wine drinkers are big sports fans now?" He shrugged. "I remember him being okay. Sure. I'd call him a reliable hitter."

We waited, leaning forward, as Jake stood at the plate, ready for the pitch. He swung hard and hit the air. A strike.

I heard River Grovians calling from the bleachers.

"Jake, you got this!"

"C'mon, Jake! No pressure. Take your time."

This time, Jake swung but missed the ball. I could feel the hopes of the crowd around us deflate.

Then the third pitch came. Jake swung hard and I heard a *thwack*. The ball flew toward the back fence. I sucked in my breath. Peony sped toward home base like she was being pursued by a bear. When it became obvious the ball had gone over the fence and there was no hurry, Nate and the councilman ran easily around the bases and made it home, while Elana and I stood gulping down our wine and cheered loudly, along with everyone else in our row.

At this point, Runty the River Rat came out and did a little dance, then led the crowd in "We Will Rock You," while we stomped and clapped in time.

After the next two batters struck out, the River Rats went out to the field. Nate easily caught the ball, and the first two runners were out. Then an outfielder caught a pop fly, and the inning was over.

When they were up next, the Garlic Heads managed to score three runs, when one of their batters bunted and the River Rats pitcher scrambled to track down the ball.

As the evening wore on, the River Rats continued racking up points against the Garlic Heads' three runs. We passed brownies, charcuterie, lemonade, and popcorn up and down our row. We did pull the blankets out from under us and wrap ourselves in them. With no sun and a strong evening breeze whipping through the trees, it was freezing.

Then came the fifth inning. River Rats fans felt victory was a given now since the score was Garlic Heads 3, River Rats 7. The bleachers emptied out as people decided to avoid the rush and go home early.

The batting order from earlier repeated, but this time Marla Sorenson hit a drive into the outfield and ended up on first base. Peony came to bat and hit a fly toward third base, sending Marla to second and Peony to first. Nate went into the batting practice area to warm up.

But even up in the stands, I could tell something was off.

There was confusion down by the dugout. Mayor C was pacing and scanning the field and the stands, a worried look on her face.

I leaned toward my friend Elana, as I kept my eyes glued to the field.

"Do you know what's going on? The councilman should be up about now shouldn't he?"

Elana shook her head. "It does seem like something's wrong."

The public address system turned on with a loud squawk.

"Keith Gregg, if you're in the park, please report to the dugout. Keith Gregg, please report to Coach Webster immediately."

Councilman Gregg had gone AWOL.

I watched as Mayor C turned to scan the stands. Then she pulled out her phone and put it up to her ear. She could be trying to call him. I remembered Nate talking about the councilman's odd behavior on Wednesday night. Maybe he'd stomped off, left the game. This was not going to go over well with Mayor C. Her star player taking off in the middle of the season opener? I almost felt sorry for the councilman; he probably had no idea of the hell awaiting him when he came back. I'd been on the receiving end of the mayor's wrath, and it was brutal.

I saw Mayor C talking with the umpire, gesturing emphatically. She was not happy.

Finally, she threw up her hands and walked back toward the dugout. Then she came out and talked to Nate, who was still in the batter-up area, taking swings.

The game announcer came on.

"And the game will continue without further delay. If anyone knows the whereabouts of Keith Gregg, please contact River Rats coach Corinne Webster."

Nate walked up to the plate and raised the bat. On the first pitch, he hit a foul, which flew back up into the stands, not far from us, to the delight of a group of kids who caught the ball then fought over who got to keep it.

On the second pitch, Nate swung hard, and the ball soared above and beyond the fence, toward the hedge of tall grass separating the baseball diamond from the rest of the park. I stood up and started screaming in delight. Our whole row did the same.

"And it's GOOOOONE!" The announcer yelled with relish, while a Garlic Head outfielder ran behind the fence to see if he could find the ball.

Marla and Peony ran around the bases, both of them tapping down on home plate with smiles. Nate followed them, though I noticed his face didn't display the glee of someone who'd just hit a home run.

He looked worried.

The people in the bleachers around us didn't care. They were on their feet, cheering. In our section of the bleachers, they were now stomping and chanting, *Nate the Great! Nate the Great!*

The Garlic Head player scaled the fence to come back onto the field. He held up his arms and waved them, yelling something.

Then he pointed back in the direction of the fence.

The pitcher, then Mayor C and the umpire, ran out to meet him. As they clustered together on the field, I heard the distant wail of a siren.

A few seats down, the chief picked up his phone, which was ringing. I felt my stomach sink, with a familiar feeling.

He stood up and made his way toward me and the end of the bleachers to begin his descent. Under the bright lights overhead, his face looked grey, the lines on his face tight.

"They've found Councilman Gregg, Gracie," he said, his voice low and shaking. "In the weeds beyond the fence. He's dead."

Chapter Three

What?

What had started out as a congenial outing to cheer for the hometown team had turned into a time of shock and grief.

The announcer came on the loudspeaker.

"Due to a medical emergency, gameplay will be stopped at the sixth inning. The matchup between the River Rats and the Garlic Heads will be rescheduled. Please take care in leaving your seats and walk safely to your vehicles. Thank you for attending tonight."

Elana turned to me. "How could the councilman be dead? What just happened?"

Kirk bent his head down, his hands gripped together. Suddenly, he stood up.

"I'm going down to see if there's anything I can do."

It was an understandable response from someone whose daily job was getting to the root of a problem, someone used to fighting fires. Kirk made his way down through the crowd below us, fans chattering away, probably trying to process what had just happened. Elana stared out at the field, a sad look in her eyes.

"Gracie, this feels like *déjà vu*. All I can think of is the concert last summer."

I swallowed, remembering. "Me, too."

Last summer, hometown rock star Noah Thornton Bell was murdered right before the encore to his comeback show, in front of The Riverside Saloon. The circumstances were similar: Noah's murder had happened when a crowd of River Grovians were clapping and cheering—fully enjoying themselves as they celebrated the return of a talented prodigal son.

"We don't know what's happened yet," I cautioned her. "This isn't the same situation as last summer."

I worried that this was murder. Or, maybe worse.

A sick feeling roiled in my stomach. What if Nate's powerful swing had driven the ball to hit the councilman, who'd been sulking in the area just beyond the fence? Maybe it was unlikely, but if this were true, Nate would be devastated.

The other members of our group were talking among themselves. Sam, Beck, Korben, and Eric stood up and made their way toward us along the row.

"We're going to take off now, Gracie. Beck's upset and I don't see that it makes sense for us to stay." Sam nodded, his face grim. Behind him, Beck blotted her eyes with a tissue. "Thank you for setting this up, Gracie. Sorry it ended this way. I-I'm worried."

I stood up. "I'll let you know if we hear anything tonight." I hugged Beck, who clung to me for a few seconds. "Try to relax, okay?" She nodded.

"I'll see you tomorrow at The Laughing Loaf," she said with a weak smile. "It will help me to get busy baking."

I patted her on the back affectionately. "That always works for me."

Chloe, left behind by her grandfather, followed the group. "Bye, Gracie. I'm going down to talk to Amelia. I'll probably see you at The Laughing Loaf tomorrow morning."

USUALLY, when events like this happened, I went in search of answers—which annoyed the chief, who thought I was sticking my nose in where it didn't belong.

But tonight, I didn't feel like going down to the field. I wanted to go home and see Nate when he stopped by after things finished up here.

I was still in shock, worried about Nate and the possibility that this might not be an accident, but murder.

I walked down with Elana. She headed to Kirk, who was standing with Jake Daniels and Mayor C—her face white. Her lips were pinched together. She nodded to acknowledge I'd joined them, which was a big deal considering how anxious she must be feeling now. I saw the chief standing out near the fence with Police Deputy Brad Castro. EMTs had arrived and were carrying out a stretcher.

"He walked off during the fifth inning. Just disappeared." The mayor shook her head. "He'd been angry since Wednesday, so I let him go. Thought he needed to blow off some steam and he'd be back."

"Nate talked about his outburst at practice. Do you know what it was about?"

The mayor shook her head. "He seemed mad at Marla for some reason. I practically had to pull him off her."

"He did say someone ran into his truck earlier that day," Jake offered. "And you know how he feels about that truck."

Maybe I was wired differently, or just that I wasn't a truck owner. But that didn't seem big enough to merit the intense anger Nate had described seeing.

But Kirk nodded. "That could be. He did love that truck."

Finally, the mayor shook her head. "No. That doesn't seem in line with how he was talking at practice. This seems bigger."

I looked up to see Nate standing by home plate, looking out toward the fence. His expression was dark, his face drained of color. He was not doing well.

"Excuse me, Mayor." I turned to head for home plate. She saw Nate and nodded.

I approached him quietly and put my hand on his arm. "How are you?"

He turned and wrapped his arms around me. "Guess I'm in shock." I looked up at him since he was a full foot taller than me.

"What else do you need to do here?"

"I'll need to talk to the chief," he said, a choke in his voice.

My instincts were right; he thought he'd caused the councilman's death. And if the chief was starting his investigation, he'd need to question anyone even tangentially involved in the councilman's death.

"I get that. The chief will want to question everyone on the team. You don't think—"

He looked down at me, his eyes pained. "I don't know, Gracie. What if the ball I hit killed him out there?"

"Do you want me to wait for you?"

He shook his head slowly. "Go home. If it's not too late, I'll come by your place when I'm done here."

I hugged him. "Come over. No matter how late."

For a second, I thought I saw his lip tremble.

"Yeah. I will."

I said goodbye to Elana, who was now with Kirk, talking to Mayor C. I caught her eye and waved goodbye.

It was a strange way to end the evening. We'd started out as a group, excited to see the game together. Now we were dispersed, each going our own way after the evening's bizarre, tragic event.

As I passed the dugout, I saw Peony sitting by herself on the dugout bench, scrolling through her phone and drinking a Diet Coke. She wasn't hanging out with the rest of the team, and there didn't seem to be any friends or family with her.

"Peony, you did a great job tonight." I took a seat near her on the bench.

She flashed me an annoyed look. "Thanks."

"I didn't know you played softball. Did you play in school?"

With her baseball cap and braid, she looked more like a middle schooler than a twenty-something professional. She sighed and looked at me with the same bored expression I saw every time I went into City Hall.

"Yeah. On my high school team. When Mayor C found out, she kept bugging me, and so, hey"—she gestured around her with a grim face—"I'm here."

"You like it?" I asked.

"Yeah, I mean, it's fun to be doing it again. Everyone on the team is super nice. Tonight, with what happened with the councilman–I mean, it was a shock."

"Did you notice he was missing?" I asked.

"He walked off during the fifth inning after he struck out. Went for a walk around the park. Mayor C went after him, then let him go. I thought it was weird, but he'd been such an ass at practice on Wednesday, we were afraid to say anything to him."

"Was that normal for him?" It would be interesting to hear what she thought of Keith Gregg, since she saw him coming and going at City Hall most days of the week.

"He wasn't usually that angry." Then it looked like she remembered something, and she snorted to herself. "He had other issues."

That caught my attention. "What do you mean, Peony?"

She shrugged and shook her head. "Never mind."

I raised my eyebrows. "When he got angry, did he say anything about his truck?"

Peony frowned. "No, why would he?"

"Somebody said he might have been mad about his truck being hit."

"The guys around here and their stupid trucks." Peony muttered. It made me wonder if she had some personal experience in this area.

I studied her face. "Are you okay? I know you worked with Keith. Can I give you a ride home?"

"I've got my car." She played with the end of her braid and stared vacantly out at the field. "I'm leaving soon, unless they're gonna ask us questions." As I stood up, she looked up at me and said almost begrudgingly under her breath, "Thanks, Gracie."

As I walked back to my car at The Laughing Loaf, I wondered about the possibility of Nate's home run causing Councilman Gregg's death. My boyfriend was a sensitive soul, especially when it came to causing pain to others, probably because he'd endured so much of it himself. I could see the burden he was carrying right now.

Could his hit have killed Keith Gregg?

I'm sure my father could run through a series of physics equations and tell me the likely speed of the ball, taking into account the temperature and air resistance. He'd calculate the force it delivered when it encountered a human being— and tell me if this could have happened.

That was assuming this was just a horrible accident.

Back at home, my father was sipping a brandy in his easy chair, Biga curled up in his lap.

I told him what had happened at the game. He didn't know Councilman Gregg, so that made it easier for him to reduce the situation to a physics problem.

He did say such a hit was possible, but that the chances of someone being killed from a long distance hit like that was very low. He wanted to go into much more detail about it, but I told him I was tired, and that Nate was coming over after he finished up—and could he *please* not tell Nate about it either.

I lay on the couch, cuddling with Biga. I dozed off for a half hour or so, tired from my early baker's hours. By that time my father had gone to bed, and Biga, the little turncoat, followed my father into his room, deciding he'd rather be in a nice cozy bed than on the couch.

At 11 p.m., I heard a tap on the door.

Nate stood there, his eyes red and puffy. I invited him in and shut and locked the door.

He held me close for a while, and I felt his heart pounding. He'd been at Grove Park for almost three hours after the game ended. I worried about what he'd tell me.

I worried about what he'd found out.

He let out a breath that felt like he'd been holding in all night.

"It wasn't the ball, Gracie. The chief took me aside and told me—this was a stabbing. Councilman Gregg was murdered."

Chapter Four

Nate slept on our couch, and I curled up with a blanket in my dad's easy chair.

Biga must have known one of his favorite people was here, because around midnight, he wandered out of my dad's room, jumped up onto the couch and settled in between Nate's legs.

At 4:45 a.m., I got up, showered, and got dressed for work. I found a clean apron in the dryer and set out lime coconut scones on a plate for Nate. I wrote him a note and filled up the coffeemaker in case he needed a jolt of caffeine to get going once he woke up.

Biga was still asleep with Nate. They looked so adorable I decided to let my little dog stay home. If he started to get annoying, my dad could call me to come get him at lunch.

I usually love driving to the bakery before the sun rises. I feel like the morning belongs to me alone, and I have the privilege of seeing it first.

Today, because of what happened at the game, the darkness felt bleak and scary. There'd been another murder in

River Grove, and the streets of my small town didn't feel friendly and welcoming at all.

Someone out there had brutally killed Councilman Gregg. Were they still around?

And worse yet, was the killer someone we knew? Maybe the killer had come into the bakery, talked and laughed with friends—and had appeared to be just like any other member of our close, friendly community.

I flicked on all the lights as soon as I got into the back room. I locked the door behind me.

I even went up front and turned on all lights in the counter and dining area. It felt warmer, safer that way.

Then I turned the sound system on in the back room and started cranking some jumpin' pop songs from the 1980s. The goofier the better.

Beck came in at 6 a.m., looking tired and troubled. She set her wicker basket of eggs from her chickens on the table near the door and hung up her jacket.

"Good morning, Gracie." She tried to manage a smile, but it wasn't convincing at all.

"Were you able to sleep?"

"My mind wouldn't shut off. I didn't fall asleep till an hour before I was supposed to get up."

I nodded in commiseration. "Pretty hard to get to sleep after what happened." Beck and Sam usually got the scoop on anything happening in town from Deputy Brad Castro, Sam's good friend. "Did you hear any news from Brad?"

Beck tied on her Laughing Loaf apron. "He told Sam that the councilman was stabbed. Looked like he was killed not long before they found him." She pressed her trembling lips together, trying not to cry.

"Nate came by last night and told me the news." I told

her Nate had worried that the ball from his home run hit had killed Keith Gregg.

Beck shook her head as she pulled the tub of beignet dough out of the fridge. "I can't imagine what that must have felt like, Nate thinking he was responsible."

"He's relieved. But he and the whole team are feeling awful about what happened. They were ready to play and were pretty sure they'd win the game. They should have been celebrating."

"I was having so much fun—until the news about the Councilman, anyway." Beck sliced dough into strips and then squares, which would become light and pillowy beignets when fried.

We'd be talking about what happened last night for days, so I decided to focus on other things.

"It was nice to see Eric and Korben last night." I turned the oven to preheat, to bake cinnamon rolls and scones, then dumped a cold tub of cinnamon roll dough out on the floured table so I could roll it out. "Korben reminds me of you."

Almost involuntarily, Beck's mouth turned up in a smile. "He talks a lot, like me. He likes to bake, too. Yeah, I'm probably closer to him than any of my other brothers. Eric's closest to me in age, but he's always kept to himself. He would have been very happy to be an only child and not have five noisy siblings."

I smiled as I slathered the butter, cinnamon, and brown sugar filling over a rectangle of dough. "I was an only child. It definitely had its advantages."

I kept moving this morning, which kept my thoughts off last night. Without Maeve on the weekends, we had less coverage with the breads and at the front counter. We had to keep things going in the back room and still be ready to engage with customers.

Many customers came in after having been at Friday night's softball game.

Jake and Jeanne Daniels were there shortly after I opened. Both of them looked exhausted.

"Hi, Gracie. We're gonna need triple shot lattes this morning," Jeanne said, leaning over the counter. "And give us two of those big cinnamon rolls. We need the sugar, too."

I gave them a sympathetic smile.

"Our heads are still spinning," Jeanne said, while Jake stood behind her, looking withdrawn and grim, his eyes shaded by his San Francisco Giants baseball cap.

"We thought it might do us some good to come in here and be with everybody else," she said.

That made sense in theory, but as I glanced around the dining room, most people in the room looked listless and down.

Even the children seemed strangely quiet, occupied with reading books or slowly unwinding and eating their cinnamon rolls.

"It probably helps to be together." I passed them their lattes and plate of rolls. "Even if everyone's feeling the same."

I looked out the bakery's front window. The flag hanging over City Hall across the street had been lowered to half-mast.

I wondered if we'd see Mayor C today. She'd probably stayed late at Grove Park last night. The chief certainly had; I didn't expect to see him. When we had a lull, I'd go over to City Hall to see who was there, if anyone.

There was a new influx of customers mid-morning, and things didn't slow down until 11 a.m.

I felt my phone buzz in my apron pocket.
I smiled when I saw the text from Nate.

> Eating delicious scones and playing a few rounds of chess with your dad. Losing is a great distraction. XOXO

I had deserted Nate this morning and left him fair game for my dad, who was thrilled to see that a chess opponent had magically materialized in his house overnight.

When business was slow enough to leave Beck by herself, I took a carrier of drip coffee and wrapped up some scones, cinnamon rolls, and a fried egg on a slice of sourdough—since I suspected the Chief would be in.

As I crossed the street, I saw Deputy Brad Castro pull open the big green door to City Hall.

Bag and carrier in hand, I went in a minute or two after him.

Peony wasn't manning her desk on the weekend, so I headed down the hall toward the offices. From the looks of her dark, tidy office, it didn't look like Mayor C was in. I heard the chief talking to Brad in his office at the end of the hall.

"Even if we found the weapon, what are the chances we'd find fingerprints? The sprinkler system goes on at 10 p.m. and any evidence would be gone at that point."

I cautiously rapped on the half-open door of the chief's office.

"Hey, chief—I brought some sustenance. I figured you'd be busy today."

"Gracie, come on in."

Brad opened the door, wearing an Iron Maiden t-shirt and smelling like he hadn't had a shower in a while. I saw the chief slumped in his chair, poring over a series of photos, dark circles under his eyes.

"Is that Laughing Loaf coffee?" His eyes widened with excitement.

"It is—and your usual egg on toast, if you're hungry."

I brought in the bag and set it down on his desk with a fork.

Back in December, the chief's doctor put him on a no-sweets diet, ending a serious addiction to Beck's beignets.

The chief looked up at me with gratitude as he began eating.

"Gracie, I don't know what to say. You came at just the right time."

"There's scones and cinnamon rolls, too, Brad, if you're interested."

I poured two cups of coffee from the carrier and set them down on the desk along with a small container of creamer.

"Both of you must have been up late."

Brad and the chief nodded, and in the next few minutes, I saw each of them surreptitiously stifle yawns.

Motive check here: Was this delivery a gracious thing to do for two hardworking members of law enforcement who stayed up late on an investigation?

Or was it an attempt to butter up the chief and Brad in order to get the inside scoop on the Keith Gregg murder case?

Honestly, I wanted to do something nice for the chief, since he'd seen the councilman every day at City Hall. But my goodie delivery did end up finagling me some information. The murder had piqued my interest, and as always, my brain was already engaged in trying to figure out how it had happened.

"How late were you two at the park?"

The chief grunted and looked at Brad. "What was it? 2 a.m.?"

Brad poured cream into his cup. "More like 2:45, Chief. Remember we did a section-by-section search of the picnic area where we found the councilman."

I inserted it in the conversation casually. "Find anything?" I asked, innocently.

The chief shook his head. "But I'm not too surprised. Whoever did this worked quickly and got away quickly."

"Nate told me that Keith was stabbed."

"With a hunting knife, judging by the cuts. They were-- unusual. That's what the EMTs said, anyway." Brad picked up a coconut lime scone out of the bag and sniffed it suspiciously.

The chief leaned his chair back on its hind legs precariously, his usual position when he was in deep concentration over the facts of a case.

"The councilman must have been caught by surprise," he said. "He didn't see it coming, but then it was getting dark. No scream. Maybe the assailant chose to strike at a time when the crowds were cheering to cover the sound."

"Nate said the councilman had gotten into a fight during practice on Wednesday. The mayor said she almost had to pull them apart."

The chief raised his eyebrows. "We interviewed everyone who was there at practice. Everyone on the team was on the field or in the dugout during the time of the murder, based on the estimated time of death." He sighed with frustration. "Everyone's accounted for."

Brad frowned. "The perp may not have been associated with the River Rats at all. Today we're looking into his personal life, to see if there was something going on, some connection we don't know about."

I remembered what Peony had said to me about the councilman last night— about his "other issues."

I wondered what she'd meant.

"Well, I've got to get back to the bakery, since it's just me and Beck today."

"I sure appreciate you thinking about us, Gracie," the chief said, taking another gulp of coffee.

Before I turned to leave, I looked at the chief.

"By the way, thanks for reaching out to Nate and making sure he knew the cause of death."

The chief bowed his head in a nod.

"I could tell he was worried he'd done something. I have to say, that was a hell of a hit. I hope to see that kind of batting again this season."

WHEN I GOT BACK to The Laughing Loaf, Beck was making drinks for a short line of customers, chatting them up as she cheerfully pulled espresso shots on the machine. If she was feeling down about last night, you wouldn't know it.

"So Marla, how's business at Spinnetti's? I heard you got some new machines in the self-service area."

They chatted as Marla talked in her low, quiet voice about the new machines they'd just installed. By the time Marla got her coffee, she looked lighter, and the lines on her forehead had softened. Beck had that effect on people.

Kirk Schiffer stood in line, scrolling through his phone. Beck greeted him with a smile and wrote down the complicated order for him and Elana, just to make sure she got it right.

"So, Elana wants hers extra hot, with two shots and light on the hazelnut syrup—is that right?"

In so many ways, Beck was The Laughing Loaf's biggest asset. Not only did she invent recipes that were a hit with our customers, but she also brought a genuine cheer and friendliness to the bakery. On a day like today, that made everything better.

"Hey, look at you," I said, as I slid behind the counter. "There you go cheering everyone up."

She blushed and looked like she was going to cry. "When I talk to people, it makes me feel happier. Does that make sense, Gracie?"

"That means you're an extrovert." I smiled. "Seriously, that's what this place needs today."

She went back to the espresso machine, as I started helping the next customer—Janet, owner of the Clip and Curl salon.

"Hey, Janet. How's business today?"

"Not great." Janet sighed, playing with one of the five tiny gold rings in her ear lobe piercings. "I'm closing early. Three appointment cancellations today. Nobody's in the mood for a cut."

"I'm sure that's temporary, right?"

"Yeah, but I can't afford to lose any business. It better pick up soon."

I pulled a kale tarragon frittata out of the display case for her and wrapped it to go. Beck set down Janet's chai latte on the counter.

"Thanks, Gracie." Janet leaned toward me and lowered her voice. "I know you talk to the chief about things. Do you know what happened to the councilman last night? Was it murder? Do they have a suspect?"

I shrugged. I didn't feel comfortable sharing details that the chief and Brad had told me. "I'm hoping the chief will issue a statement soon, so we can all know what's going on."

Janet eyed me shrewdly, as if she were trying to figure out whether or not I was keeping something from her.

"Well, I hope he does that soon." She took her chai and frittata and headed for the front door. "It doesn't help any of us sleep at night, knowing there's another murderer out there."

When we closed at 2 p.m., Beck made us each a coffee drink, and we chilled in the back room for a few minutes. I hadn't eaten lunch and I suspected Beck hadn't either. I brought back the remaining items from the display case, and we took what we wanted.

"I didn't even get a chance to think about the renovation today. It's coming fast." I picked up an apple tart from the tray and sliced it in half. Beck took a kale frittata and grabbed a napkin.

I wanted to bring up what was currently obsessing me: what we'd do while The Laughing Loaf front area had to be closed for two weeks—or more.

After all, it might help to focus on something that wasn't murder.

"This is a completely different topic, but can I pick your brain about something?" We both started in on our tarts. "Turns out we will have to close the front area for at least two weeks while the contractors work on the counter and dining area. I want to do a pop-up version of The Laughing Loaf—and set up to sell our pastries and breads somewhere in River Grove."

"Where could we do it?" Beck sat back on her stool at

the table. "When people do a pop-up, it's usually in an empty space somewhere, isn't it?"

"It could be. I can't really think of any space here in downtown." I lined the cinnamon rolls up in a baking tray. "I mean, the Loudon Antiques Emporium next door is convenient—and vacant—but that place still creeps me out." I'd had a run-in with a killer there last year, and I still had flashbacks of the cold, damp air and mildewy smell.

"I wouldn't want to sell baked goods in that place." Beck shuddered.

Nate had seen pop-ups in LA set up in or alongside other businesses. I tried to think of any in town that might be a fit with The Laughing Loaf.

"Corner Market has a patio on the side that's sheltered." I tried to picture the space.

Beck frowned. "Yeah, but it's really small. I don't think we could fit much there, let alone the two of us to sell things." She was silent for a while, as we both worked. "What about The Riverside? Do you think Reggie would let us set up there?"

"I'd thought about that. I don't want to take away from Reggie's business—or get in his way." I looked out the back door at the blue sky and the trees rustling in the breeze. "But what do you think about using the green-space in front of The Riverside? You know, where they hosted the summer concerts last year. It'll be spring and as long as the weather stays nice, people will want to be outside."

"We could set up a booth under a tarp or canopy," Beck said, as she took a bag of herbs from the fridge, to chop for the kale frittata filling. "Coffee could be a problem, since we can't run an espresso machine out there."

"So we'll set up Cambros and serve drip coffee for the

weeks we're there," I said. "It's better than not having coffee at all."

"We can still bake here, and transport everything over to the greenspace." Beck said, as she brought out the big pot for frying beignets and heaved it onto the stove. "It could be a lot of trips, but it won't be too bad."

"I'll talk to Reggie and see if he's good with this. I've been playing around with a streamlined menu for the pop-up, to make things easier. We can talk about that when Maeve gets back on Monday."

After mourning and speculating on Keith Gregg's death, it felt good to look ahead to the future. The renovation would bring a new era to The Laughing Loaf—lunch service, a new dining area, and probably more customers. It would be a lot of work getting to that point.

Right now, at least, it seemed like it would be worth it.

I woke up at 4:45 a.m. the next morning, and the first thought in my mind was: *Let's get this pop-up thing settled.*

I rolled out of bed, but Biga, who'd been wedged in against my leg all night, didn't follow me.

He watched me get up, shot me some side-eye, then laid his head back down on the covers and closed his eyes.

"Fine. If you want to stay home, go ahead." I muttered to him. "But no lunch time walk. And good luck with getting attention from Papa today. He'll be busy prepping study guides for desperate students."

Biga opened his eyes, then stood up and jumped down to the floor.

I showered and dressed, then pulled a load of clean Laughing Loaf aprons out of the dryer to take with me.

"So, you're in, Biga?"

I opened the door of his crate, and he went in without a fight.

We went out to the car for our daily drive to the bakery.

I was feeling better about the darkness this morning, with some distance from Friday's murder.

The early morning darkness can be beautiful. Even a comfort during stressful times.

In River Grove, it was cold, crisp and full of sounds that you could hear only if you tuned in: birds with their first morning chirps, the hooting of owls, the San Luciano River gurgling over rocks on its course to the ocean, and the random snaps and cracks the forest makes when it's in the process of waking up.

Once I got in the back door of the bakery, I settled Biga in his pen. I turned on all the lights and put on some energizing retro pop music.

My brioche and white biga loaves were rising nicely in the proofer. It helped that Maeve had taken on many of the bakery's bread duties. She was handling most of the sourdough and the basic whole wheat loaves and would get new batches started when she came in tomorrow.

I finished slicing a roll of cinnamon roll dough with a sharp knife, and the cinnamon butter filling oozed out between the slices.

When it comes to phones, I'm more of a texter than a caller. So, I texted Reggie McFerrin to ask if he'd be up for having a Laughing Loaf Bakery pop-up on the greenspace in front of The Riverside.

Saturdays and Sundays at the bakery felt very different than our more hectic weekdays.

We opened an hour later than we did on weekdays. Customers came in relaxed, not in a rush to grab coffee before their commute to Silicon Valley or in a hurry to open their businesses in town.

The crowd was usually small: couples with their dogs, parents pushing toddlers in strollers, and people who wanted to linger in the dining room over board games or conversation. Everything came down a notch, and I usually worked at a relaxed enough pace to have conversations with customers.

Before we opened, I set the Laughing Loaf Joke of the Day in its stand. I'd worked hard to find baseball/softball jokes in preparation for the season opener, but this weekend, I skipped those. I'd stick to more generic subjects.

Laughing Loaf Joke of the Day
I gave my handyman a to-do list, but he only did items 1, 3, and 5. Turns out he only does odd jobs.

I was working in the back room when Beck popped her head in the doorway. She gestured behind her, to the front counter.

"She's *here*." She whispered. "Mayor C."

I hadn't expected to see Corinne for a few days. She'd been hit by the loss of a coworker and one of her best players.

I went out front and met her at the counter. She looked pale, and—if this word could ever be applied to Mayor C—frail.

I saw no sign of her usual energy, gruffness and sarcasm.

"Good morning, Gracie." She said quietly. "I'll have a large oat milk latte and the kale frittata."

"Good to see you, Corinne. I'm so sorry for what happened Friday night."

"Thank you, Gracie." She checked something on her

phone. "Make this to go, please—I'm going back to City Hall. Dave's going to brief me on the investigation. Then I'm going to call a special meeting tonight for the team, so I can share the progress on the case with them."

"Good idea, Corinne." The mayor felt a strong sense of responsibility for her team, similar to the responsibility she felt for her town. "Any news from the councilman's family?"

The mayor looked taken aback by the question. "Why do you ask? Everybody knows he was in the middle of a divorce. Keith moved out and was living by himself in a condo in Los Gatos. I did call to express my condolences to his son, Emmett. He goes to UC Santa Cruz."

Maybe everyone else had heard about his divorce, but I hadn't. But then the councilman wasn't a regular at The Laughing Loaf. The only time he'd come into the bakery was when he couldn't get his gas station coffee last week, and that hadn't been a great interaction.

"I didn't know Keith very well," I said, as I passed the mayor her frittata in a bag. "I'm sure it's a big loss to River Grove and to the River Rats."

The mayor took a deep breath, a look of despair on her face. "I thought this was the year we'd win the championship. We had the talent."

Not that this was the moment for it, but I wanted to reassure her that she had other good players on her team. There was Peony, who was a surprise asset, and Nate.

"I was surprised to see Peony playing on the team." Beck passed me the mayor's oat milk latte. "I never would have thought of her as a softball player, but wow. She's really good."

The mayor nodded as she picked up her latte. "I'd been asking her to be on the team since we hired her. I found out she was a star player in high school—up in Marin County. She finally agreed to give it a try."

"Nate's enjoying being on the team," I said, not adding that he was relieved Mayor C was putting less pressure on the team, after his pre-season injury.

"He was born to play sports, that man." Mayor C shook her head slowly, as an almost dreamy smile lit up her face. "Nate is a fine specimen of manhood indeed."

She took her latte and frittata and headed for the front door.

From the espresso machine, Beck gave me a look halfway between shock and a suppressed giggle.

"Did I hear that right? Did the mayor just say your boyfriend is a fine specimen of manhood?" She whispered.

"Yes, she did." It felt so good to laugh. "And I know enough about Corinne to realize that her *only* interest in Nate's body is that it will help her win this year's Mountain-Coastal League championship."

THAT NIGHT, my fine specimen of manhood called at 9 p.m. on the dot to tell me how the special practice-update went with Mayor C.

"She told us they haven't found any trace of a knife in the park. All of us team members were in the dugout or stands when Keith was killed. So, they're looking for another angle to pursue."

"When Corinne came into the bakery today," I said, "She told me the councilman was in the midst of a difficult divorce."

"Huh. That's news to me. Keith wasn't a talkative guy. I don't think I heard him share anything personal." Nate paused. "No, I take that back. He did talk about his son in college."

Pieces and little tidbits of information floated around in my head—clues I'd picked up from listening in the last couple of days. They were like tiles for a mosaic that might eventually form a picture. I might assemble these things at some point—if I was at all interested in working on this case. Right now, the renovation loomed large in my mind, ready to take over my life. I hated that I couldn't know exactly how long it would last. Or when we would re-open. Would it be three weeks as the contractor promised? One month? Or—please, no—*two* months?

Nate and I wrapped our call up by setting a date to get together on Wednesday, once he'd finished a photo shoot at Elkhorn Slough, a wildlife sanctuary on a swampy estuary near Monterey.

I was lying in bed, thinking too much about everything going on right now—when I got a text from Reggie at The Riverside.

> Yes to the pop-up in the greenspace. We have a canopy that should work.

> Let's talk—come by tomorrow.

Finally, something out of this week's chaos was settled. My mind was at ease, and I slept soundly all night.

Chapter Five

I woke up Monday morning at 4:15 a.m., before my alarm even went off.

Biga popped his head up to give me a *what-the-hell-is-this* look then dove back down under the quilt.

"Biga Boy, don't give me that look. You're coming with me today whether you like it or not. We'll take a walk at lunch today to see your favorite person—remember Reggie?"

Biga looked at me as if seriously considering his options. Then he hopped down from the bed.

I set out my clothes and got ready.

I was up early enough that I even made some *pre-coffee* —from the drip coffeemaker—that would get me to work so I could enjoy a delicious latte made by Beck on the espresso machine. Pre-coffee was a pale brown liquid that only vaguely resembled the real coffee I'd get later. But it had enough residual caffeine to get me moving.

I carried Biga out in his crate and we took off on the dark streets of River Grove. The air was moist and cool today, which made me wonder how we'd handle the pop-up if it rained. I'd ask Reggie about this today.

Beck and Maeve came in at the same time today, so Maeve could get up to speed on this week's bread bakes.

"How was business at Pain Parisienne this weekend?" I asked, as Maeve watched the stand mixer churn a batch of country sourdough.

"Wine tourists came in by the droves. The weather was beautiful. We were packed all weekend."

"You heard what happened Friday night?"

Maeve nodded soberly. "Corinne told me when I got back from Napa last night. She's lost a really good player. And she worked with Keith. I think she's trying not to show how sad she is."

No surprise to me. This was the mayor's MO.

"Maeve, Beck, and I were trying to find a spot for a Laughing Loaf pop-up, since we'll have to close the front area for two weeks. Looks like we've got one."

"That's cracking." Maeve brightened, using the British colloquial term for *awesome*. "Where's it going to be?"

I told her about The Riverside's greenspace, and Reggie's response that we could do it there and he'd provide us with a canopy.

"So, we'll be outdoors in spring. That sounds perfect. So much more fun than staying inside."

"There are some logistics we'll have to figure out—like how to transport baked goods and coffee from the back room to the pop-up throughout the day." I slid the first of two trays of cinnamon rolls into the oven. "We'll need to work on that."

"This sounds great. I'm in." Maeve heaved the stand mixer bowl onto a metal table to begin forming loaves.

Beck looked up from the hot oil where she was frying

beignets. "What if we came up with something that we bake just for the pop-up?" She had that look in her eye—her creative mind was already envisioning something. "A special treat we don't serve here. It might bring more people out to the pop-up."

"I love that idea," I said. Customers would be willing to come to the pop-up if they could get something they wouldn't normally get at the bakery.

"Brilliant, Beck." Maeve said, as she used a bench scraper to separate a loaf from the bulk dough. "If you want to brainstorm ideas, we could do happy hour at The Riverside."

Beck looked up immediately. "Really, Maeve? I'd love that."

"If you can, let's go after we close."

"Let me text Sam and make sure it's okay," Beck said, uncertainty in her voice. "It would be fun to come up with ideas."

I was excited and proud that this was becoming a collaboration—and that my two employees were becoming friends.

"One thing to think about, though. Whatever you come up with will sit for a while at the pop-up. Beignets and anything fried need to be hot and fresh, so they're probably off the menu."

Maeve nodded. "We will take that into consideration."

Before we opened, I set out a new joke on the stand. These jokes were goofy—very much dad jokes—but I'd already seen people laugh this weekend when they read them. If a joke could cheer customers up during this hard time in River Grove, I was going to keep putting them out.

Laughing Loaf Joke of the Day
My dog accidentally swallowed a whole bag of Scrabble tiles.
We took him to the vet to get him checked out.
No word yet...

The high schoolers came in, looking as though the weekend's murder hadn't dimmed their high spirits. They were joking, laughing, and sharing things on their phones as they nabbed spots at the dining area tables.

When Amelia Gruber came up to the counter with her friend Dakota Li, I smiled.

"Great job on the national anthem. That's got to be hard. It's just you out there. No accompaniment."

Amelia beamed. "I was really scared. I sang at my little brother's soccer tournament once, but that was in front of, like, 30 ten-year-olds."

"You so nailed it," Dakota gave her friend a side hug.

Chloe came in with Jeb, one of my father's Physics students. For the past few months, the two had been sitting together by themselves at a table in the dining room. They couldn't be more different: Jeb was academically driven and uptight. Chloe was a laidback hippie, and occasionally punk, version of a cheerleader. Both of them looked quite serious today.

"I'll have the usual—chai latte and a cinnamon roll," Chloe said.

"And I'll have—the same." Jeb gulped, adjusting his glasses. He hadn't ordered this before. This was interesting.

"Only a few weeks now till the AP test. My dad said you're doing really well in the prep sessions."

Jeb turned pink. "Mr. Markley makes it so easy to understand. I just hope I can remember it for the test."

I set their drinks and cinnamon rolls out on the counter.

I watched as the two made their way to a table at the back of the dining area.

Was I a snoop, just as Police Chief Westerman said?

Yes, I was. I might ask Chloe later whether they were a couple—which would be an interesting twist considering she couldn't stand Jeb just two months ago.

After the crowd of high schoolers made their noisy departure, heading down the street to River Grove High School, we had just a few minutes to wipe down tables and regroup before the older crowd came in, usually around 8:15 a.m.

The chief came up to the counter by himself, no sign of his partner in crime, Mayor C.

"Good morning, Chief. What can I get you this morning?"

"Drip coffee with some cream and *The Chief*—as you're calling it now." He smiled sheepishly. We'd named the egg on sourdough after him since we'd invented it to accommodate his new diet. It wasn't really on the menu. I could tell he really liked that we named it for him.

I nodded at Beck, and she called back to Maeve to get the chief's order started.

"Corinne came in yesterday," I said. "Sounds like the past few days have been tough on her."

"She's supposed to meet me here soon." The chief angled his head toward the window. "She texted me that she has a few questions about the investigation."

"I was wondering, Dave. I never really got to know the councilman. Do you have a few minutes to tell me a little bit more about him?" I was surprised this even came out of my mouth. I must have been thinking about the case.

The chief looked behind him to check the line. The bakery wasn't packed yet. And Mayor C wasn't here.

"I guess so," he said. "If you've got a few minutes,"

I went to the drip coffee maker and poured him a cup, then set out the creamer full of half and half. I asked Beck to cover the counter for me.

We went back to the corner table, which was River Grove Public Safety Central for the chief and the mayor. For the past year and a half, the two had met here nearly every weekday morning to discuss crime, traffic, and murder in River Grove—that is, apart from a weeks-long falling out they had last year over an arrest.

"How long had Keith been on City Council?" I asked him. "Looks like he's been here since before we came to town."

"Keith was on the council for eight years. Since River Grove is so small, members of the council are elected informally during town hall meetings every four years. He was active in a few committees—recreation and education. No one else wanted to serve in the position, so when Keith said he'd do it, everyone was so grateful, they voted for him."

"Nate said his main job was selling insurance. What has he done in his role as councilman?"

The chief wrinkled his brow as he thought.

"The mayor knows more than I do about it. I guess he worked to get the speed limit reduced on the highway into town. He helped us get upgrades to the Grove Park stadium."

I'm not sure I'd call the Grove Park baseball diamond and aging bleachers a *stadium*, but I'm sure it was better than it looked before the upgrade.

"Was he well liked?"

The chief tilted his head. Then he snorted.

"Well, not by his wife. Other than that—" He sat up as he remembered something. "Oh, yeah."

I leaned forward. "What is it?"

"Now I remember. This was years ago, before he became councilman. He fired his office manager, then she took him to court and sued him for unlawful termination. She lost."

"Is this person still living in River Grove?"

"Oh, sure." The chief nodded. He glanced over at the counter, probably to see if the mayor had come in yet.

"You probably know her. She's on the River Rats. Her name's Marla Sorenson."

Chapter Six

A jolt of electricity shot through me as I heard the name.

At the same time, I looked up to see a line forming at the counter. Beck was telegraphing me a nervous look: *You really should be behind the counter now.*

"Chief, she got in that fight with the councilman at practice last week. It was intense. Mayor C had to pull them apart."

I nodded to Beck and started to get up.

"I've got to get back to work, but right off the bat, it sounds like Marla could have a motive for murder."

The chief shrugged. "That might be, but the mayor said Marla was in the dugout at the time the murder occurred."

As I stood up, Mayor C was coming through the front door of the bakery.

"Anyway, thanks, Chief." Even as I headed back, I wanted to pursue this subject further. "I'll talk to you later."

I took my place at the counter, as the line grew longer—and the customer requests got more ridiculous.

"Medium latte, please, Gracie. And can I have two

dozen of those coconut lime scones to take home to my family?" I glanced at the case to see we only had six left.

"I'm so glad you like them. But I can only give you six. You're welcome to put in an order tomorrow for two dozen, if you like."

The next customer:

"I heard you're going to be serving lunch. Can I get a sandwich now?"

Then a young woman came up to the counter looking so shy I was afraid she was going to cry. Her wavy hair was piled on her head, pinned up with a pair of ornamental chopsticks. She looked familiar.

"I w-was wondering if you're accepting job applications."

I smiled and took in my breath. We'd need to hire help for our lunch service—and we needed to have people ready and trained by July. Sooner than that, we'd need basic help with the pop-up.

But I didn't have applications ready to hand out.

"Can you come back at 5 p.m? We can chat then." I wished I could make her less scared. "And what is your name?"

"Rose. Rose Wilkins. Yes, I can come back at 5."

"Come to the back door—right off the alley behind the bakery. Our name's above the door. You'll see it."

She took a deep breath and her entire face lit up. "Thank you. You're Gracie, right?"

I nodded. She walked out, it made me feel good to see, without the fear she came in with.

It was almost noon. I needed to get over to The River-side to talk to Reggie about the pop-up.

The line at the counter had died down now, and Beck was cleaning up at the espresso machine.

"You okay if I go meet with Reggie about the pop-up? I'm taking Biga with me."

"Things will be slower now." Beck sighed as she cleaned the machine's spout. "Unless people think we're *already* serving lunch."

I rolled my eyes. "I know. Ha. I wish we could fast forward through the renovation and get straight to the serving lunch part."

I went to Biga's pen off the back room and snapped on his leash. He was very ready to go for a walk. I texted Reggie to let him know I was coming, and we took off.

The sky was clear and blue today, and the air smelled fresh, clean and woodsy. Biga was thrilled to be out of his pen. He was so happy to be outside, he had to visit every single bush and pole on our way. It took us a while to get to the saloon.

Reggie stood on the front porch of The Riverside to meet us. When Biga saw him, he tugged on the leash. Reggie bent down to greet him.

Reggie McFerrin had run The Riverside Saloon for the last forty years. According to my River Grove friends, he'd converted it from a hippie commune he founded in the 1970s. Reggie wore shades during the day and lived a nocturnal lifestyle as he ran the popular bar and music venue by night. With his long, jet-black hair and pale, waxy skin, when I first met him, I thought he looked like a vampire.

I couldn't always decipher Reggie's mysterious, almost poetic way of talking, but his kindness and offbeat wisdom got through to me. When I'd first met him, I didn't get it: why did everyone in town adore this guy? It took a while for me to get to know him, then I understood.

"Biga, I haven't seen you in a while." The saloon owner

brushed the top of Biga's head. The dog closed his eyes, happy. "Have you been behaving yourself?"

"No, he has definitely *not*." I laughed.

My dog began licking Reggie's hands and standing up to paw at his legs, trying to do anything to get closer to him.

"I'm sure he'll let you pick him up, Reggie."

The music venue owner scooped him up and held him in his arms, much to Biga's delight, as we walked out to the greenspace.

"I was thinking of the area closer to the street, but still near the benches—so people could have a place to hang out. We can bring our own chairs and tables, but I don't want to have to set up and take down things every day."

Reggie nodded. "You shouldn't have to. You're going to have enough to bring over from the bakery. We have some metal chairs and outdoor tables in storage. It won't be as big of a seating area as you have in the bakery, but it should be fine for a temporary set up. And there are benches nearby."

"Thank you so much for all this, Reggie."

Biga rubbed his head against the man's neck. He'd be perfectly happy to live in a baby sling on Reggie's chest for the rest of his life.

"Want to try setting up the canopy to see if it'll work for you?" Reggie set Biga down and took out his phone. He called his assistant Bryce and bartender Marty to bring out the canopy and a long foldable table.

Meanwhile, Reggie and I scouted out the best spots on the green. When we chose a spot not far from the street, Bryce and Marty set up the canopy, made of a white nylon material and an aluminum frame. It was faster to put together than I thought.

Reggie and I erected the long portable table in the canopy. It would serve as our counter. I'd bring tablecloths and a smaller display case we had in the bakery's storeroom to finish the setup.

I'd ask Marcy, owner of River Grove Printing and one of our regular customers, to make us a sign to post on the canopy. I hadn't even thought of that, but it would draw people to the pop-up and let people know that we were the bakery down the street, now temporarily selling on the greenspace.

Afterwards, Reggie and I sat on a bench on the greenspace, Biga in Reggie's arms, looking over at the canopy. I took a few photos on my phone to show Beck and Maeve.

It looked like this was going to work.

Now I felt a surge of excitement instead of dread. This could be a fun, new way to interact with our customers. I looked forward to offering Beck and Maeve's special menu item.

Reggie looked thoughtful.

"Gracie, the biggest problem will be the connection between your baking room and the pop-up. You'll need to hire someone to help with that. You can't do it yourself. I know you're running a tight operation, and you have nobody to spare. There will be a lot of running back and forth—and you'll need to have good communication with whoever's back at the bakery."

I knew that, of course. On weekdays all of this would take place during school hours, so hiring the students, as we'd done for Valentine's Day deliveries, was out of the question. I wondered about Rose, the young woman who was coming back for an interview at 5 p.m.

I'd have to think about this, in the twelve days we had before The Laughing Loaf closed for renovation.

And with everything else that would happen in the next few weeks, that would fly by fast.

. . .

Rose Wilkins came to the back door at 5.

I brought her up to the dining area.

"Can I get you an espresso drink, Rose?"

Her eyes widened with delight. "Can I have a latte? With oat milk, if you have it."

I'd found a tablet of applications in the storeroom, so I peeled one off the pad and had her sit and fill it out.

Meanwhile, I made her a latte.

By the time I brought back her drink, she'd written up her job experience, which was two jobs. She'd graduated from River Grove High last year.

"What made you want to work here, Rose?"

She smiled shyly. "I love your bakery. I remember when you started here, and I would come in. It became my happy place. I'd get coffee and a cinnamon roll and sit near the window and read."

Now that she said it, I did remember the quiet girl with the slightly crazy hair who sat by the window reading books.

I looked over her experience. "Since you graduated, you worked at a fast food place in Santa Cruz then a thrift shop. What made you leave those jobs?"

She turned red and cleared her throat. "I learned that I really don't like fast food, so I quit. The thrift shop was a nice place to work—I loved organizing the clothes and meeting customers and working the register, but it went out of business last month. I worked there for a little less than a year. I've been looking for another job since."

I asked her if she'd be interested in working with us as we did the pop-up by The Riverside. She could transport baked goods on the cart from the bakery to the pop-up. I'd hire her for this period of time at first. If it worked out both for her and for us, I'd bring her on permanently to work the register and train on sandwich and food prep.

"You'd start in two weeks. And you'd be working with us at the pop-up, until we can move into the renovated space here at the bakery."

"I've always wanted to work at The Laughing Loaf. I've spent a lot of time here. I'm willing to do anything."

"Okay, Rose." I smiled as I took her application. "Why don't you come back next Thursday, and I can show you around. You can meet our bakers, Beck and Maeve, and learn more about how this will work."

"Really? Thank you for giving me a chance, Gracie." She clasped her hands together and beamed.

I had a good feeling about Rose. She'd start out doing one, unglamorous job—hauling stuff back and forth between the bakery and The Riverside pop-up. If she could do well with that one thing, she could be given more.

I returned to the back room.

Maeve put loaves into the proofer for the overnight rise, and Beck filled two trays of tarts for baking tomorrow morning.

I wiped down work surfaces and set up a load of dishes to wash in the super speedy Hobart dishwasher.

I went to my small cubby of an office to open any mail in my slot. All I had was an invoice for the upfront payment on the renovation and several catalogs for kitchen equipment. I paused to look at a catalog for ovens. I wondered about getting us a new oven in addition to the refurbished oven I'd started the bakery with. Then I leafed through the pages and saw a combination mode oven that leaped off the page like a pinup girl would leap off the page for a 1940s sailor.

It was sleek and roomier than what we had. It had

several modes of cooking and baking, which would accommodate Beck's pastries, lunch menu foods, and, with some prep for us to learn the settings, all of our breads.

With something like this, we wouldn't have to block out our baking schedule so tightly. We'd have capacity to bake more and flexibility for what we could bake and when. I shoved the catalog into my tote bag. It would cost money—a lot of money.

Beck and Maeve were finishing up. I took off my apron and put it in the used bin. I took Biga's crate into his pen. He went right in, eager to get home.

"I'm heading out now. Lock up, stay safe—and have fun at happy hour, you two."

They looked up, their cheeks flushed by their work in the back room. They looked so giddy, young and excited for their night out, they made me feel old, even though I was only 32. Maybe I felt the smallest tinge of jealousy. Elana was at a work event tonight till 8 p.m., and Nate was at his photo shoot at the slough.

"See you, Gracie!" Beck called.

I heard the two throwing out baking ideas, some of them intriguing—and some just plain ridiculous.

THAT NIGHT, I made a quick dinner for my dad and I—a steak salad, a concession to my dad's deep love of steak. With dinner, I served a tempranillo I'd bought at a wine shop, after enjoying Elana's at the game.

My father cleared his throat.

"Gracie, what do you know about resumes?"

I snorted as I poured dressing on my salad. "What's going on? Are you looking for a job, dad?"

"No, but Mary Jo is. She wants to apply for a part-time job. Something in Boulder Creek."

"But she already runs the nursery." I sat back and studied his face. I was intrigued by this news. "Why does she need a part-time job?"

My father wiped his face with his napkin. "She said she's found something she very much wants to do."

"Okay." That wasn't a whole lot of information to go on. "I hired people in my management job in Seattle, so I know what makes a good resume. I don't have a lot of time right now but tell her to call me. We can go over what she's got."

My father gave me the sweetest, most grateful look. "Thank you, dear. This means a lot to me. I know you haven't always liked Mary Jo in the past."

I sighed. "That's not exactly true. I didn't know her well, and to be honest, I compared her to mom. I'm learning to appreciate her for who she is."

"She thinks quite highly of you, Gracie. I'll tell her to call."

After dinner, as my father dutifully rinsed dishes and loaded the dishwasher, I lay on the couch with Biga and texted Elana.

> Do you or Kirk know much about Keith Gregg?

Then I pulled out the catalog and began looking at ovens again. This was developing into an obsession.

I called to my dad, who was loading the dishwasher.

"Dad, is it a bad idea to spend $12,000 on an oven?"

"What? For our kitchen?" He responded through the clinking of plates. "I would say that's a bit pricey, dear."

I laughed. "For the bakery. It would help us bake more and have more flexibility with what we bake."

My father came in from the kitchen, a dish towel over his shoulder.

"How can I put this?" He tilted his head and took in a deep breath. "Dear, you are a penny pincher. If the oven will benefit The Laughing Loaf, maybe you should think about spending the money."

Is this how people saw me—a cheapskate? Was I as bad as Councilman Gregg, complaining about the outrageous price of scones and coffee?

The Laughing Loaf was bringing in customers from Santa Cruz and San Jose. Reviewers were saying good things about us. We were making a modest profit.

But Reggie had mentioned it today. I ran a very lean operation.

We were growing beyond the capabilities of our existing equipment and staff. As we expanded to include lunch service, we'd need to invest in equipment and staff if we wanted to continue to make a profit.

Penny pincher or not, I needed to attend to that.

Chapter Seven

I dozed off on the couch.

I woke when my phone buzzed against my face.

I peeled it off my sweaty cheek and looked at the text.

I texted back sleepily and monosyllabically.

Half an hour later, she knocked on my door.

Since my dad was in his study, she came in and plunked herself down in his easy chair.

"Oh my God, Gracie. That party was so boring. They had no right to call it a party." Elana threw her head against the chair back. "When I saw your text, it was my excuse to leave. Thanks, girl."

I reached for my water bottle and took a gulp of cold water to wake up.

"I want to know all there is to know about the councilman. When he came by the bakery last week, he was rude and mean—but maybe he was just having a bad day. But the more I hear from people, the more weird vibes and comments I get."

Elana looked intrigued.

"Tell me what people are saying." She leaned closer, in the way that she did when she wanted to hear all the gossip, which was quite often.

I sat up, cross-legged on the couch.

"First of all, Nate told me that Marla Sorenson and the councilman almost got into a fist fight at last Wednesday's River Rats practice. Then I heard from the chief that Marla worked for Keith's insurance business years ago. He fired her without giving her a reason, and she took him to court. She lost."

Elana's eyes were big. "I have not heard this."

This next thing was pure hearsay, since I hadn't gone back to Peony to have her explain further. I needed to do that. Peony wasn't my favorite person, but if she knew something about the councilman from working at City Hall with him, I wanted to hear it.

"After the game, when I asked Peony if she'd ever seen the councilman that angry, she said, 'No, not that angry. But he has *other issues*.'"

"What other issues?" Elana asked, narrowing her eyes.

"She didn't say. I need to ask." I sighed and continued. "And... apparently the councilman was in the middle of a bad divorce with his wife."

"Oh, *her*." Elana nodded, new understanding in her eyes. "I know Karen. She's an interesting one."

"Please tell me more," I took another glug from my water bottle. "Why is everyone saying it's a messy divorce?"

"Okay. Well, first of all, Keith Gregg is—*was*—obsessed with money. He's the guy who volunteers for everything then makes sure he gets money out of it somehow. He agreed to be councilman because nobody else wanted to do the job, and he turned it into a way to promote his business. When he worked to get the speed limit lowered downtown, he turned it into a way to sell car insurance. He raised funds to re-do Grove Park Stadium then he plastered the dugout and stands with ads for his business—"

"But is it *really* a stadium? I mean it's just a baseball diamond with bleachers."

Elana gave me a silencing glare. "Gracie, it's what we've *got*."

"So Keith used every opportunity to promote his business." I said, relating somewhat to the business side of this. I owned a small business, and Elana did not. "That's a tacky move, but it doesn't make him deserving of murder."

"I'm telling you what kind of person he was because you asked," Elana said. "Keith's goal was to make money. Their house—which Karen's living in now—is on Oceanview Drive near us. It's 4500 square feet and gorgeous. No expense spared."

"So she got the house, and he moved into a divorced dad's apartment," I said with admiration. "She must have had a good attorney."

Gregg's story was getting interesting. And I wondered—if the councilman's goal was to make money at all costs, where else had he gotten money? A house that big here in the mountains was expensive, even if it wasn't in the heart of pricey Silicon Valley. What if the councilman had embezzled funds from the town coffers? Or made money off the town in some other way?

"Karen did get a good attorney. All those years of letting Keith indulge himself got to her, apparently. She was trying to take him for all he was worth."

"And he's dead now, so she gets all of it."

Elana nodded. "Well, Karen and then their son, Emmett, who's in college."

Granted, I was hearing all of this from Elana, who had her opinions. But it sounded like the councilman hadn't been the public servant he'd made himself out to be. Instead of serving the public, he helped himself—to any opportunity to make money.

A chill ran through me as I realized: this was what my ex-husband did. Ben loved money. And when he saw the chance to make lots of it—so he could buy a beautiful house, a tricked-out sailboat, and anything else he wanted—he used his security clearance at work to sell defense secrets to foreign governments. When I confronted him, he told me he had no problem with it. He worked hard at his job, and this was a bonus he gave himself. "The technology should be free to everyone anyway," he said, rationalizing it all.

I started to feel sick to my stomach.

I remembered that when I'd talked to Mayor C about Keith Gregg, she hadn't mourned his loss as her co-worker in town government. She was sorry to lose a good batter who could have helped the team win the league championship.

I wondered what she thought about him as a person. It was always a little tricky talking to the mayor about these things—in fact, it was tricky talking to the mayor about *most* things—but if I was going to figure out why this murder happened, I'd need to do it.

"Any wine left from dinner?" Elana asked, peering in at the dining area where the bottle of tempranillo stood on the table.

"If we do, you shouldn't have any." I said reprovingly. "You still need to drive up the hill to your house."

She sighed. "I guess you're right. I'm feeling a little cheated by tonight's event, that's all. I mean, seriously. You don't go over spreadsheets at a party."

I was still feeling a little sick that Councilman Gregg reminded me more and more of Ben. I saw my ex-husband's face, that smug look he had that last night in Seattle, when he told me he could easily take me down with him. He'd tell the FBI I'd been involved in the scheme.

How had I ever believed this guy loved me?

How had I managed to block him out of my mind since then?

I tried to focus on my conversation with Elana. I wanted to get as much information about Keith Gregg as I could from her.

"Okay, now back to the councilman," I sat up and took another drink of water to ease my stomach. "If you had to choose based on what you know, who do *you* think killed him?"

Elana leaned back in the recliner, just as my dad walked down the hall to the kitchen. I saw the horror on his face, as he stopped in his tracks and saw someone daring to sit in his special chair. But his Brit dislike for making a scene won out. He pressed his lips together and continued to the kitchen.

"Well, Karen has a motive—she gets all his assets, and her son and all his college bills are taken care of. And she doesn't have to have the guy around."

"Marla Sorenson is a possibility, too," I said. "But the

chief told me she was in the dugout during the time Keith was supposedly killed. Also, the lawsuit against Keith was a long time ago. What would make her kill him now?"

"We could blame the Garlic Heads," Elana said with a sigh, crossing her legs and luxuriating even more in my father's chair. "Maybe they knew if they got rid of the River Rats' best hitter, that was their one chance to win."

I lay my head back against the couch. I'd been up since 4 a.m. and was now feeling both exhausted and nauseous. "Nate says they're not a great team. Even if they got rid of our star hitter, they'd still lose." I gulped down more water.

Elana gave me a curious look.

"Girl, are you okay? You don't look good. I'll get home and let you sleep. We need a girls' night out sometime soon."

"Always up for that." I stood up uneasily as Elana got up out of the recliner. "Thanks for all the info."

"Sure thing, G. Just fill me in on anything else you find out."

As I saw Elana out and locked the door, I went to the bathroom to see if I was actually going to throw up. Nope.

Then I checked my phone for the usual 9 p.m. text from Nate, who was still down at the slough for his shoot. He'd sent me a sort of homemade postcard, a beautiful picture of a snow white heron in a grass-filled swamp with a cursive headline across it:

Greetings from the Slough
Wish you were here!

I told myself I'd lay down on the couch for just a few minutes till I felt better, then go to bed.

The next thing I knew, it was 4:30 a.m. I looked around the room, completely disoriented.

I was still lying on my side on the couch, Biga curled up next to me.

I'd dreamed I was in the house in Seattle with Ben, and he'd just told me he'd been selling secrets for the past four years of our lives together.

It felt so real, I thought I was actually still there. And that all of my time in River Grove—with The Laughing Loaf and Beck, and with Nate—had just been a dream.

My throat felt choked with unshed tears. Biga nestled closer to me.

If I could, I wanted to talk to Karen Gregg today.

Chapter Eight

After a large cup of pre-coffee, I drove to the bakery, Biga in the backseat in his crate.

Today I needed to focus on the bakery and the changes we had ahead of us.

I debated whether or not to talk to Beck and Maeve about buying the new oven.

I decided I'd do a little more research, talk to some bakers using it, and tell my staff about the oven if I decided to buy it.

When Beck came in, she preheated our current oven and brought out the tarts she'd assembled with Maeve. She was working fast already, this early in the morning. Her dinner out with her coworker seemed to have energized her.

"Maeve and I had so much fun last night. We talked about *everything*. She told me about the pastries they make at Pain Parisienne. And she showed me pictures—they look beautiful," Beck said breathlessly. "They look like *art*. I'd love to take a French pastry course if I can find one."

Last fall, I'd given Beck a generous stipend for her education fund. It was an investment in The Laughing

Loaf, since as soon as my talented assistant learned a technique, she tried it out by creating a new item for our menu. She'd taken a few courses at baking institutes and bakeries in the Bay Area.

Now a dark look came over her face. Her cheeks looked flushed.

She seemed upset, worried about something. Then I realized it looked a lot like guilt. Which for sweet, naive Beck had me a little scared.

What trouble had she and Maeve gotten into at The Riverside?

"Gracie, last night—" She swallowed and looked down. She lowered her voice as if she were about to confess to murder.

"I had—" She swallowed then blurted it out, "—A glass of *wine* with my dinner."

Now I need to explain something about my assistant here: Beck grew up in a very sheltered home, where alcohol wasn't allowed. From what she'd said, Sam didn't drink, either. Beck lived in a world completely different than the one I'd grown up in. Her friendship with the more sophisticated Maeve might be opening her up to some new experiences. That wasn't a bad thing.

But I didn't want to laugh at Beck or in any way make fun of her. She was a kind, devoted employee, whose joy and exuberance made The Laughing Loaf the welcoming place it was. She had just taken a step out of her comfort zone. She was miles away from Elana and me as far as wine consumption, but for her, this was a big deal.

I went to the fridge to take out the tub of cinnamon roll dough which had risen nicely overnight.

"So you had a glass?" I smiled back at her. "What did you think of it?"

"Maeve said maybe I should start with a sweet wine. So I got a Riesling."

I smiled. "Ooh, Riesling's good. Did you like it?"

"It was like dessert." Her brown eyes turned soft, as she moved on to filling another tray of tarts. "I would totally have it again. It made me feel giggly." She looked nervous and quickly said, with a firm shake of her head, "—but not like I was *drunk* or anything."

I melted butter in a pot on the stove and stirred in cinnamon and brown sugar.

"Would Sam get upset that you drank alcohol?"

She slid the first tray of tarts into the oven. "I told him when I got home. He said it was my decision whether I wanted to drink or not."

"Good answer." I turned around and smiled at her. "That's what I'd expect Sam to say."

"Gracie, I haven't had a lot of women friends. Kids from homeschool families mostly, and they were all from here in the mountains. I grew up with five brothers. I like that Maeve's my friend. She's so different from me—and she's really fun."

"That could be a good thing, Beck. For both of you."

Beck sighed, a wistful look on her face. "I laughed more last night than I can remember. Sam's great. But I don't really go out and have fun, you know, with *friends*."

I wanted to encourage this. Not like there was an age requirement for fun, but Beck was twenty-three. She didn't have kids. She gave 150 percent to her job at The Laughing Loaf. She should be having a little fun in her life. "Let's have a night out some week night. You, Maeve, me, and Chloe Westerman, if she wants to join us." Chloe often filled in at The Laughing Loaf. Beck had become her baking mentor.

Beck's face lit up. "I'd love that."

"Hey, did you and Maeve come up with any ideas for the special menu item for the pop-up?"

Beck laughed and clasped her hands together. "We came up with *way* too many ideas. We decided we need to do a baking night to try some things out. Maybe tomorrow night or Thursday." She went back to slicing up the beignet dough. "I know we need to get it set for the menu and be able to order ingredients. I was thinking—since we won't have beignets or French Toast Sticks at the pop-up, it would be nice to have another breakfast item."

"Great thinking," I said as I spread rectangles of cinnamon roll dough with filling. "And I can't wait to taste test whatever you come up with."

Right before we opened the door to the high schoolers, I set the joke of the day out on its stand.

Laughing Loaf Joke of the Day
I kept wondering why the baseball
was getting bigger. Then it hit me.

Mayor C came right after the high schoolers left, to get coffee and a kale frittata. She looked a little hardier today. There was color in her cheeks and life in her eyes.

She read the joke of the day and snorted.

"Nice one, Gracie."

I pulled a frittata out of the case and plated it for her.

"Hey, Corinne, there's another River Rats game this Friday, right?

She nodded. "We're sticking to our schedule, and we'll make up last Friday's game when we can set a date with the Garlic Heads. Friday we play the Los Gatos Gopher Trappers—on their field. They're actually pretty good, so we may be at a disadvantage without—"

The mayor stopped and shook her head. Beck put the mayor's oat milk latte on the counter. I wished I could ask her how she really felt about the councilman, but there were customers in line and now wasn't the time.

"I bet it will be a challenge going back there, Corinne. But you've been preparing for this for so long. You've got a good team. And lots of crazy River Grove fans."

"They get a little wild, don't they?" the mayor said with an affectionate smile. "For years, even when we didn't win, they kept coming to games."

"They know you're the one who changed that." I smiled. "I hope you keep doing it."

The chief came in not long afterwards, asking if he could order drip coffee and "The Chief" to go.

"I'm interviewing a couple of people this morning," he said, lowering his voice. "Corinne's one of them. I trust her observations. I need to hear more about what she saw Friday night—now that some of the shock is gone."

"You just missed each other, Dave. I think she was heading back to City Hall."

"I want to respect her time to grieve," he said in a soft tone I rarely heard from him.

"She was doing much better than when I saw her last." Maeve came out from the back room and set "The Chief" down on the counter with a smile and quick wave at the actual chief. "For what I just saw of her, Corinne should be okay with answering questions. She may want to help out now."

The chief studied my face. "You think so? This has been tough for her."

"And you're right. Corinne is observant. She could be helpful."

"Karen Gregg is also coming in," he said grimly, taking a sip of his coffee. "I don't know what to expect from her."

I was curious to meet the councilman's wife—or should I say, widow.

I was wondering if Elana would be up for making a neighborly visit with me soon, to the Gregg house on Oceanview Drive.

I ENDED up meeting Karen Gregg sooner than I thought I would. She came into The Laughing Loaf to get coffee about an hour later, before her appointment with the chief.

I didn't know who she was at first—I only noticed when she paid for her coffee and beignet. I saw the name KAREN GREGG pop up when she inserted her card into the pay station.

She was a petite woman in her fifties, who probably worked out, judging by her fit figure. She seemed confident, not somebody I'd picture putting up with the councilman as I understood him.

"Good morning, Karen. I'm sorry to hear about your loss."

Her head snapped up after she'd just signed her name.

"What?" She turned fierce, wide black eyes on me. "My *loss?* We were in the middle of a divorce. A divorce that should have happened a long time ago."

I shook my head as I listened. And I just went with it. I spoke, for the most part, my truth. But I played it up a bit.

"I get it, Karen. I've been there. I was married to a real loser. I know I should have left sooner."

She put her wallet back into her purse. "The worst

thing is, I can't get all the crap he left behind out of my head. His schemes. His lying. He cared for two things. Money and himself. He was a narcissist."

So Keith Gregg had been a *lot* like Ben. I nodded in genuine commiseration.

Karen Gregg was still standing there at the counter, and a couple of customers had just entered the front door.

I was getting good info here and I wanted to hear more.

I nodded at Beck. "Will you be okay if I chat for just a few minutes?"

She'd been listening to our conversation. She smiled and gave me a thumbs up.

"Karen, I'm taking a quick coffee break. Wanna talk?" I picked up my very lukewarm latte from early this morning and headed toward the dining area.

"If it's short." She looked down at her Apple watch. "I've got an appointment with the chief in about 15 minutes."

She followed me back to the corner table, which was appropriate since this was an interview, even though it sounded more like a group counseling session for two disgruntled ex-wives. The two of us were bonding—and quickly.

I leaned across the table, playing the part of the supportive confidante. "Were you at the game on Friday night?"

Karen sighed.

"I *never* went to his games."

"What a shock, though, that Keith was killed—I was at the game, and I still can't believe it happened."

She slapped a hand down on the table.

"And that's what I mean. The man's dead, so I have no closure. Nothing can be addressed now. I'm stuck with all the baggage he left me with for the past twenty-five years. Granted, I did inherit quite a bit of money, and Emmett did, too. I guess that's something."

I sighed. "My ex actually did some illegal stuff to get money. And I didn't find out for a while."

Karen stared at me as she took a sip of her coffee. She lowered her voice. "I wouldn't put that past Keith. I always wondered. I know he took advantage of people, and probably cheated them, but I never really had proof."

I tried not to look surprised.

"Oh, I'm so sorry, Karen."

"We used to be happy." She sniffed a little, as she pulled out her wallet. She showed me a photo of her younger-looking self, next to a muscular young man, with a full head of dark, curly hair, big dreamy grey eyes, and an engaging smile. I couldn't believe this was the same person as the balding, hunched over man who'd complained about the high price of our coffee.

"That's *Keith*?" I looked at her in shock.

She nodded.

My first thought was that Keith Gregg was like Gollum in *Lord of the Rings*, a normal person twisted into a slimy, deceptive creature by his obsessive desire for a ring—or in Keith's case, money.

She slid the photo back into her wallet, a nostalgic look on her face.

"He tried out for a minor league baseball team. Almost made it, too. Keith was really good. He'd gone to college on a baseball scholarship, and he wouldn't have gone otherwise. His family was dirt poor." She looked down at the table, thoughtful. "Which was part of his problem. He never felt he had enough."

"How does your son feel about Keith?"

Karen looked at me wryly. "Emmett's smart. He knows. He wasn't shocked when I decided to divorce his dad. He never asked why. He said, 'Don't worry. I've got your back, mom.'"

Her features softened into a smile for the first time.

"I should get over to City Hall. I needed to talk to somebody, and you were right here at the right time." She stood up and turned to me. "I never got your name."

"Gracie. Gracie Markley," I said, rising from my seat.

"Good luck with your situation, Gracie. I hope it works out for the best."

I didn't tell her, but I was sure it already had.

When I went back behind the counter, Beck gave me a funny look.

When she set the next espresso drink on the counter, she smiled like she'd just been let in on a secret.

"That was sneaky," she whispered gleefully. "It sounds like you *are* on the case."

"Maybe. Though it's not a great time with everything else going on."

"It's never a good time, though, is it? We'll never not be busy. We'll never not be dealing with something crazy."

I laughed. "Beck, you are speaking the truth."

Chapter Nine

I went to work in the back room to get brioche loaves ready for tomorrow's bake. Maeve was doing a final proof for the country sourdough, which would be going into the oven soon. She needed to get the loaves baked this afternoon so we could use the oven for everything else tomorrow morning.

She put on a playlist of Irish and British pop. I'd heard it before. It was growing on me. I started singing along, too, under my breath, as I tried to figure out how to get some information out of Maeve.

"I'm curious as to what kind of oven you use at Pain Parisienne. Do you have multiple ovens?"

"Just one convection oven. Since we're still pretty small. It's new, though." She gave me a sly look. "Why do you ask?"

"No reason," I said with a smile. "Just curious."

"Would you be thinking of getting us a new oven? Because if you were, Gracie, that would be great. We really need one. I'm sure they're very expensive."

I raised my eyebrows and smiled mysteriously. "I'm trying to figure some things out."

AFTER A NICE WALK with Biga over to the greenspace at The Riverside, I deposited my dog in his pen and sat down at my desk.

I found the number for the oven manufacturer's local office and called to ask if they had any local installations—or bakers willing to talk about their experience with them. They gave me some names and numbers.

I had zero time to do this research right now, but I might be able to make a few phone calls in the next week.

If we were doing a renovation, and we also needed to upgrade our oven, we might as well do it as soon as possible. It would make our time in the pop-up easier.

I thought about my dad calling me a penny pincher.

I tried to figure out how that had come about.

And the more I thought about it, I started to see that this stinginess started when I married Ben.

Ben spent extravagantly. He'd tell me he'd bought a top-of-the-line fitness system and it was going to be installed next week in our den. On impulse he bought two tailored Italian suits—which, unfortunately, he looked amazing in. Once, he came home and announced that we were going to Africa that fall to hike Kilimanjaro, and all the arrangements were first class.

When he did things like this, I instinctively cut my spending. I was afraid we were spending too much. So I scrimped and cut corners. It became a habit.

I found out the truth one night, months later, when I opened a folder on his computer. He'd been keeping huge sums of money in separate accounts—all from foreign governments.

I had a feeling that Keith Gregg wasn't selling defense secrets to the Russians or taking in anywhere near the amounts of money Ben had.

But he'd been doing something to get money, something that allowed him to live a posh lifestyle in this small town while continuing to look like a humble public servant.

His cash surplus couldn't just have come from the fact that he bought his morning coffee from the gas station instead of The Laughing Loaf.

Karen Gregg seemed to be telling the truth when she said she wasn't sure what Keith had done to get his money.

But there was somebody who might know.

I needed to figure out a way to talk to him.

Chapter Ten

It was 4:30 p.m. and we were closed when Mayor C knocked on the back door of The Laughing Loaf.

Beck and Maeve were finishing up so they could grab appetizers at The Riverside and come back to do their baking/testing session. The music was blaring, and they were singing along. Loudly.

I asked them to turn down the music.

"Sorry, Gracie!" Beck called out from metal table where she was slicing bread for tomorrow's French toast sticks.

I turned to the mayor. "Let's go up front to the dining area."

She followed me, but she walked so fast, I hung back and let her lead.

"Corinne, what's up?"

"I need to talk to you, Gracie." She looked stressed.

"Can I get you a drink?"

"Water, please."

After she took a seat at the corner table, I went back to get her a bottled water from the fridge.

"What's going on?" I looked across at her once we were

seated. Lines had tightened into parentheses around her mouth.

"It's the Runty mascot costume. It's nowhere in the storage shed. It wasn't found at the stadium. Anywhere."

I shook my head slowly. "Okay. And why is that important?"

She frowned at me. "The Runty costume hasn't gone missing in the fifty years of River Rats softball."

"So it's an important part of town history. But isn't the murder we're dealing with a little more important?"

She continued. "Luke Robbins, who played Runty at the game, doesn't know where it is. He took off the costume during the fourth inning to go to the concession stand. He left it in the dugout. When he came back, it was gone."

I started to see what she meant.

"So you think someone wore the costume to kill the councilman, incognito."

The mayor flashed me a *well-it's-about-time* look. "If the killer was wearing the costume, there could be blood, hair, DNA on it, that could identify the killer."

Could this be true? That night during the game, a large rat had roamed Grove Park after dark, armed with a knife.

Something Elana said about Runty at the game Friday nagged at me, but so much had happened since then, I couldn't bring it to mind.

"You told the chief the costume's missing."

"He had the same reaction as you did, Gracie--*Yeah, so what?*"

I decided to be up front with Mayor C, since she was always that way with me.

"Things are very busy here right now. Tell me what you want from me, Corinne."

"I want you to find out who took the costume." The

mayor pressed her lips together firmly. "Find them and you'll find our killer."

I leaned across the table. "Corinne, can I ask you a question?"

"Go ahead," the mayor said gruffly.

"It seems like you've been more upset about the loss of your star batter—than for River Grove losing a councilman."

The mayor's mouth twitched. She nodded reluctantly. "I always suspected Keith was in it for himself. From way back. Some things have happened lately that made me think he was embezzling from the town."

I raised my eyebrows.

"How?"

"Off and on, the past two years, our recreation and maintenance funds have gone missing. Peony's in charge of these. They're in a locked drawer in her desk until she takes them to the bank in Los Gatos. Actually, we only started locking the drawer recently—and unfortunately, that's just us, being a small town city hall. It was never a problem before. Peony's been very upset. I think you know how seriously she takes her duties."

I *did* know, from personal experience. Was this the "other issues" Peony talked about the councilman having?

"We have no proof." Mayor C shook her head. "The chief couldn't come up with any either. We bought a security camera for inside the front office. It was supposed to be installed this week."

River Grove was a small town. If Keith Gregg was going to embezzle, how much could he really get?

"Does this really add up to much?"

"That's usually been 500-600 a month." Mayor C said matter-of-factly. "It's a big amount for our town budget. We have a big rec program compared to other towns our size.

And when we lose that money, it makes it harder to pay instructors for the rec classes or do maintenance on things like the stadium and Grove Park."

Why hadn't I heard about this? Maybe it was embarrassing for the mayor to admit this theft had happened right under her nose.

"Thank you for answering my questions." The mayor prepared to leave, and I stood up. "I'd like to help if I can. Let me think about it."

As I walked into the back room, Beck and Maeve were laughing and chatting as they put on their jackets to go over to The Riverside for appetizers. Nate was out of town on his shoot, and my dad had tutoring tonight.

I felt a twinge of loneliness inside, a desire to tag along with them. But even if I saw myself as one of the "good" bosses, I'd still be the boss, going to dinner with her staff. They'd be less guarded without me, and they'd have a lot more fun.

"Enjoy yourselves," I called out to them. I'd rescued Biga from his pen and gotten him into his crate. "Can't wait to see the treats you come up with."

"See you tomorrow, Gracie," Maeve called.

"And don't worry," Beck said with an excited grin. "We'll make a big mess for sure, but we'll clean it up before we leave tonight."

It was still light outside, one of those warm spring evenings where kids ride bikes and play games outside, enjoying a preview of a summer with no school. I drove home with Biga, thinking about my talk with Karen Gregg, and how our bad husband experiences had bonded us into instant confidantes.

And wondering if Mayor C was right—the person who'd taken Runty's costume was the councilman's killer.

The past four days, I'd been going about my days at the bakery, as I made cinnamon rolls, layered scones, and studied specs on new ovens—thinking about the murder and a lot about Councilman Gregg. This is how my mind works: I see something broken or out of place, and it nags at me. My mind works overtime trying to put it back together, make it right again.

I puzzle over it, just as I did when I worked at my job in tech and had to troubleshoot a software bug.

I had a strong feeling that Keith Gregg's murder was related to who he was as a person. My talks with Karen Gregg and the mayor gave me more confidence in that theory. I needed to think about this more.

Maybe a quiet house was what I needed tonight.

Chapter Eleven

After feeding Biga, I took him out in the backyard and let him run around and get some exercise.

"Okay, Biga boy. What about a walk in Grove Park?"

As usual, the word *walk* immediately got him excited. He jumped up on my legs, spun around in circles, then headed to our front door.

Since it was a couple of miles from our house, past downtown, I decided we'd drive to the park, then walk. I didn't want to be caught as the sun went down, now that I had a picture in my mind of a large, knife-wielding rat stalking through the park.

Since it was still light and warm outside, the park was packed. Kids scrambled over the playground equipment near the entrance, creating a bottleneck at the big slide, which looked like the biggest attraction on the playground. Parents watched and talked to each other on the benches.

After I parked, I took Biga out of his crate, leashed him, and we walked around the park in the direction of the "stadium."

In the distance, a group of pre-teens were playing a pickup game of softball on the diamond.

As we got closer, I looked over at the picnic table area beyond the ballpark fence. Tables at other parts of the park were full, but these were empty. Probably because word had spread that the councilman had been killed just a few feet away.

I walked past the tables, examining the long strip of tall grass that grew just behind the low ballpark fence, a sort of natural barricade between the ballpark and the rest of Grove Park. Part of it was flattened, like somebody'd forged a path through it—probably the first responders on Friday night.

I looked toward the ballpark from this vantage point, trying to imagine Keith Gregg standing here, looking in at the dugout, the mayor, his teammates, and the people in the stands.

I wondered what Keith Gregg had been thinking about. What had he been running away from out here? Had he heard his killer approaching him?

Biga and I made our way around to the dugout. The kids were a group of three boys and a girl. They were taking turns pitching and hitting, or at least trying to. When someone got a hit, the batter skipped, walked backwards, or crawled on all fours around the bases while the rest of the players stood and watched, doubled over with laughter.

Biga and I watched for a while, then walked around the stands, at least until Biga found a cardboard boat of old French fries under the stands and made a run for it.

I pulled him away.

The dad of some or all of the kids walked out to the diamond.

"Time to go home, guys."

The kids moaned, and the feisty one on second base screamed. *Noooo, Daa-aad!*

"Come on, guys."

The dad looked over at me. "Hey, you're from the bakery. Gracie's your name, right?"

"That's me. And this is Biga, my dog."

"I'm Phil. Phil Wakeman. You at the game Friday? Geez, that was bad, huh?"

I shook my head. I remembered my confusion that night. "I saw that something was going on by the fence. But I couldn't really see what."

"We were just above the dugout," the man said. "After a while, we figured somebody'd been hurt out there. We guessed it was the councilman, since they just announced he was missing."

Maybe Phil and his family had seen more than I had, since they were closer to the dugout.

"Since you were so close, I'm curious about something— did you by any chance see the mascot Runty go into the dugout during the game?"

"Runty?" He waved again at the kids, who were taking their sweet time coming in. "Yeah, he did go into the dugout. Maybe the fourth inning? Didn't notice that he ever came out, though."

Which would make sense because Luke Robbins took the costume off and went to the concession stand.

"After that, did you see anyone come out of the dugout holding something—maybe in a bag or box?"

Phil rubbed his forehead and thought about this. "We were all on our feet cheering like crazy. We didn't win like this when I was a kid. So my eyes were on the field. I wasn't even looking at the dugout then."

I smiled at him. "Thanks, Phil. I was just trying to figure out something."

"Dang it, Ty! Get the heck back here now!" Phil yelled at the lone kid kicking the dirt as he wandered slowly back to us. "Dinner's ready and we gotta get home. Your mom's gonna be mad."

"Nice meeting you, Phil. I like the way your kids play baseball."

"They're crazy," the man said, grinning, as two of his kids ran up and tried to tackle him. "But I think we're gonna keep them."

Watching his kids gleefully swarming over their dad brought something up in me. I couldn't stop smiling. There was something I'd shoved down years ago, because Ben hadn't wanted kids. Well, maybe now I did. Someday, anyway.

Biga and I walked back to the parking lot, as the sun started to slip behind the trees.

After all the exercise, Biga would sleep well when we got home, which was good. I wanted to do some online research.

Once we got in the house, Biga drank water from his bowl, then curled up on the couch to sleep. I found some leftover lasagna in the fridge and was so ravenous I cut a slice and decided to eat it without heating it up.

It was *delicious* cold. Everything. The texture, the flavor. Why did I not know this?

I pulled out my laptop and did a google search on Keith Gregg. I found his insurance office website. He seemed to rely on scare tactics for selling insurance.

Someday, you will die. It's reality, friends. Will your family be provided for? MAKE SURE TO INSURE! - with Gregg Life Insurance.

Which seemed ironic given his own recent demise.

There was an obituary in the Santa Cruz Sentinel which listed his successful insurance business, numerous awards from business organizations, and his eight-year-reign as River Grove councilman, where he "worked selflessly to serve the people of his town in the areas of public safety, health and fitness."

Possibly while selfishly helping himself to the coffers of River Grove.

In obituaries, you don't always see who a person really was. You see a list of accomplishments, positions held, degrees earned. It is possible for these lists to paper over who the person really was. Councilman Keith Gregg looked very good on paper. But to know who he really was, you had to talk to his wife, child, coworkers, and teammates.

There were a few of these people I still wanted to talk to – if I could manage to fit them into my pre-renovation, pre-pop-up craziness.

After closing my laptop, I picked up my phone.

I had a text message from Mary Jo.

Do you have any time tonight, Gracie? I'd like to show you my resume. You can also say no.

> Dad's tutoring. I've got some time. Come over!

Mary Jo showed up at the front door at 7:15 p.m. in a colorful bohemian caftan, her white hair pulled back in a ponytail. I gave her a hug, then led her to the dining room table.

"Thank you, Gracie." She sat down across from me and set down a folder full of papers. "Your father says you're very busy these days."

"The Laughing Loaf remodel is happening soon, so there's a lot going on." I looked up at her with a smile. "The results will be good. It's just going to be crazy for a while."

She pulled stapled sheets of paper from the folder.

"I've been thinking a lot about my life in the past month, while your father and I have been taking a break." She looked down. "When I married my late husband, I stopped doing things I loved. One of those things was the theatre. I miss it."

When my dad and Mary Jo spent almost all their time together, I'd resented her. In retrospect, it was all on me.

I got a little territorial. She used our kitchen—*my* kitchen—to make dinner with my dad almost every night. I also unfairly compared her to my mom, who'd died when I was fifteen. Then I learned that Mary Jo was an interesting woman in her own right, with a backstory I could never have imagined. She'd acted in a national touring company and in local Shakespeare productions.

"Your father is so happy now that he is back doing what he loves." She sighed. "I want to have joy back in my life, too. I won't be acting again at my age, but I want to be in the business again."

"What is the theatre company you're applying to?" I

brought out my laptop and took some notes. I wanted to help her get the job.

Mary Jo folded her hands and leaned over the table excitedly.

"Boulder Repertory Theatre, just outside Boulder Creek on the highway. It's a small company—the theatre's in an old, renovated church. They've been doing short works by local playwrights. They do a musical once a year in the summer. It's their big moneymaker. This year, they're doing *Camelot*."

"Nice." I nodded, happy for her but wanting to keep things moving here. "What's the job opening?"

"Handling mail, sending out fundraising information, making calls to businesses to recruit donors. I did the same things for a local theatre before I married Bill." Worry lines appeared on her forehead. "But that was twenty-five years ago. I don't know if it counts."

She really wanted this job.

"It does count," I said. "You've also been running a nursery for the past twenty-five years. That's good management experience, and you worked with customers and sent out mailers."

She nodded. "Every month."

"Let's mention that in your experience."

I wrote a note of these things under the heading of skills and experience on her resume.

"You didn't mention your acting career anywhere here. You were in a touring company. That shows you know the business. List the roles you've had. You did Shakespeare, right?"

She nodded. "I guess you have a point, Gracie. I wasn't sure how much I should put in." She pulled out a printed list of the parts she'd played over the years. It took up three-quarters of a page.

She started to tear up.

"I have done a lot. I forget that." She looked at me with a sad smile.

For the past year, I'd seen Mary Jo as an intruder, a cigarette-smoking, celebrity-gossip-obsessed presence in our house. She was so different from my mom, I couldn't imagine her being my father's love interest. She *had* been a little clingy with my dad. I was starting to like her, just as my dad realized that he had other interests he wanted to pursue, not just making dinner with her every night.

By the time Mary Jo left, we'd printed a resume with the changes I'd suggested. She hugged me and thanked me profusely.

"I can drop this by the theatre office tomorrow," she said excitedly, wiping a tear from her eye. "I'll write a cover letter tonight."

"Keep me posted, Mary Jo. I can't wait to hear what happens with this."

After she left, I was feeling pretty self-congratulatory about this step in my personal growth. I mean, I *had* come a long way in my relationship with Mary Jo. I let Biga out in the backyard and had a quick runaround with him, even though it was dark and a little spooky outside.

Nate was coming back from the shoot tomorrow, but I missed him. I wanted to talk to him tonight.

So I texted him at 8:30 p.m.

Still coming home tomorrow?

Nope. I've decided to make my home in the slough.

I sent him a laughing emoji.

Two minutes later, he called.

"It's not even close to 9 p.m., Gracie." He let out an exaggerated sigh. "I hope you appreciate how hard it is for me to break my routine."

It felt good to hear the amusement in his low, rich voice. I wanted to pull it around me like a blanket. I laughed.

"I miss you. Beck and Maeve are at The Laughing Loaf testing bakes right now."

"Feeling left out?"

"A little. But it's been a good couple of days. The pop-up's on track, and it looks like I have a new employee." Then I told him about my conversations today with Karen Gregg and Mayor C.

"I'm not surprised by what his wife is saying," Nate said. "He always seemed uptight, like he was focused on something else. Every conversation I had with him, he seemed to be trying to spin it toward promoting himself or his business."

I told him about Mayor C's Runty theory.

"At the park I talked to a guy who'd been at the game with his kids. He said he saw Runty go into the dugout in the fourth inning, like Mayor C said. It's possible someone snuck in after him and stole the costume."

Then I remembered—*duh*—Nate had been there. "You didn't see anyone unusual in the dugout at that time, did you?"

"I didn't. I was very focused on the game." He went quiet for a moment. "So Keith could have been killed by someone in the Runty costume? That's really bizarre."

"Like something from a bad horror movie," I said. "I was creeped out thinking about it when I was at the park tonight. I walked right past where they found his body."

"If this is true, then nobody knows what the real killer looks like." He paused. "Be careful, Gracie."

I heard the worry in his voice.

"Biga and I got back before it was dark tonight. I'm trying to stay safe, stay in well-lit areas. I don't want to be the stupid woman in the horror movie who gets killed because she goes off on her own."

"Why do they always *do* that?" Nate said. "It's like the director wants people to yell at the screen."

"It keeps the audience engaged, maybe?" I shrugged.

"Gracie, will you promise me you won't do something like that? I know you like to figure these things out. I understand that. But I also like having you around."

There was a serious issue behind his joking. His parents had died in a plane crash when he was a teenager and then his brother Nico was found dead on The Laughing Loaf's back step last year. Nate was way too familiar with loss.

"And I look forward to having you around tomorrow." I said, lightly. "Come by the bakery if you can."

"I will if I can. The slough's been fascinating, and I got some great shots. But I'm missing you, too."

"Awww." From that point, the conversation between us degenerated into a round of squishy, romantic talk. I hung up, feeling a lot less lonely.

I was also excited to see what happened tomorrow. There were a few things I wanted to follow up on. I wondered if the mayor was right about the missing Runty costume.

This had become a strange case, whether the legendary rat was involved or not.

Chapter Twelve

Beck came in to work the next morning, grinning excitedly.

She took off her jacket and hung it on the rack, then pulled an apron out of the clean bin and practically danced while she brought it down over her head and tied it.

"You look even more cheery than usual this morning, Beck." I laughed. "That's saying a *lot*."

"Maeve and I had so much fun last night. And, we came up with *three* things we think we can make for the pop-up." She skipped over to the fridge and pulled out beignet dough.

"Three? You were busy last night. Can't wait to see what you two worked on. Show me the evidence."

She giggled, then brought me her wicker basket. She took out a wrapped dish.

"Exhibit A, the macarons." She unwrapped the dish to reveal a variety of colored, perfectly smooth, round cookie sandwiches. Pink, green, purple, and yellow. They were beautiful.

"So there's strawberry, matcha, ube, and lemon. They are so good. Here, try one."

I grabbed an ube one and took a bite. The texture was perfect, with the first delicate crunch, and then the light, creamy, nutty flavor—which came from *ube*, the Filipino purple sweet yam.

As soon as I finished one, I wanted another.

"So good, Beck. Really."

"I couldn't stop dreaming of the ones Maeve showed me from Pain Parisienne. They don't do ube there, but I love the flavor of the ube scones you make, Gracie. These would hold up well out in the pop-up, too."

I had to resist grabbing another macaron to try all the other flavors. "What else do you have?"

Beck reached into her basket and pulled out a wrapped plate with three muffins on it. She took off the plastic wrap and set them down on the table. "And here is exhibit B— apple streusel muffins. Perfect for breakfast. They have a yummy crumb topping, and the muffins are super moist."

She handed me one on a plate. I hadn't had breakfast, so I almost drooled on the muffin before I ate it. I closed my eyes as I bit into the crumbly, buttery topping and discovered the soft, moist inside. Pop-up or not, this would be another winner on our menu.

"Again, amazing. This is delicious. We should eventually put this on our regular menu."

Beck's face shone with joy. "I'm so glad. We had so much fun doing this. And yes, I did have wine at The Riverside, and really liked it," she said, shaking her head emphatically. "But I only had one glass."

I tried not to laugh. "You know you're talking to someone who drinks a lot more wine than you do, right? Where is Exhibit C?"

Beck took a breath and looked a little giddy. "Maeve took it back to her place since it needed a longer rise. She's bringing it when she comes in. But I can't tell you what it is. She'll have to show you. She had to call Rafal a few times to ask for his help."

If Rafal, former breadmaker at Night Rose in Napa, helped with this, it must be a bread-related item. Which would probably hold up well in the pop-up, too. Now I was curious.

This was like Christmas morning: seeing the surprises that my employees had worked on last night.

"I'm grateful to you two for coming in last night to make these. How late did you stay?"

Beck looked a little nervous.

"Um, it was about midnight," she admitted, shifting on her feet as she watched me.

"I don't mind you and Maeve being here then, but I'm concerned with your safety." I remembered Nate worrying about me being outside at night in a town where a murder had just happened.

"Please be careful. I'd feel better if you didn't stay so late—and if you made sure that the two of you stuck together."

"We did! I drove Maeve home and saw that she got in okay," Beck said with a frown. "But I see what you're saying, Gracie. We shouldn't have stayed that late."

"You were having fun and being very productive," I said with a slight smile. "I get that."

Maeve came in at 6:30 a.m., a goofy grin on her face. She brought a wrapped tray into the back room.

Beck was frying up beignets, which the teenagers would devour when they came in at 7. I slid two large cinnamon roll trays into the oven. We both looked up from our work.

"Okay, Maeve, I've got to see what you made. Beck gave me a heads-up."

Maeve set the tray down and pulled a layer of foil off the top.

There lay a tray of light golden-brown focaccia, topped with cut vegetables arranged to look like a garden: chives and rosemary stems, yellow and red pepper flower petals, red onion roses, and purple potato slices. It was a work of art.

"This took a long time," she said, apologetically. "It's not perfect, but I FaceTimed with Rafal up in Napa and he helped me."

"Maeve, this is gorgeous. I can make focaccia, but I don't have your artistic eye to do the decoration."

Even though we had a lot to prep this morning in order to open at 7 a.m., the three of us couldn't stop talking about how we'd integrate these bakes into our schedule.

I'd been nervous about the beginning of our renovation, but now I had new rumblings of excitement.

I had a team committed to this.

This pop-up was going to be fun.

Just before the high schoolers came through the door, I sliced up some of Beck and Maeve's treats and set them on top of the display case as samples, to remind customers that we'd be in the pop-up soon.

Chloe Westerman, Amelia Gruber, and Dakota Li were standing in front of the case, looking at the samples.

"That focaccia with the flowers," Amelia cooed. "It's amazing."

Chloe eyed the macarons with interest.

"Ooh, what are those, Gracie? Can I have a sample?"

"Sure. We have macarons, apple streusel muffins, and

focaccia. They're going to be featured in our pop-up bakery at The Riverside."

"The macarons are so pretty. Can I have a pink one—and then a piece of streusel muffin? And my usual cinnamon roll and chai latte."

"Sure thing." I put a cinnamon roll and the samples on her plate. "No Jeb today?"

"I don't know where he is." Chloe frowned. She seemed annoyed at the question. "Probably celebrating his acceptance to Princeton. She leaned over the counter and kept her voice low. "Everyone thinks I *know*—like we're a couple or something. We're absolutely *not*. I just hang around him because he actually studies instead of talks when we come here. I'm taking my grades seriously."

My question was answered. And now I knew—Jeb had managed to get into a really good school.

"Good for you. Jeb does take school very seriously."

Chloe would be around for another year. But Jeb, and his childhood friend Sky Robbins, River Grove High's class clown, would both graduate from River Grove High in two months.

When we started opening early last year, the high schoolers drove me crazy with their noise, bickering, and occasional cluelessness. But I'd gotten used to them all and learned to love their energy. I'd miss the seniors.

My consolation was they'd be home on breaks from college and would probably come to The Laughing Loaf to meet up with old friends.

A little after 8 a.m., I'd just put another tray of cinnamon rolls in the oven, when a young man walked up to the counter to order, backpack over one shoulder. The high schoolers were still here, crowded around tables, chatting. It was noisy.

"Good morning. What can I get you today?"

He wore wire-rimmed glasses. He was around my height and looked vaguely familiar.

"I haven't been here before, but my mom told me it was cool. My class in Santa Cruz was cancelled, so I thought I'd come up here to hang out."

I studied his face. "Wait a minute—are you Emmett Gregg?" That's why he looked familiar. I could see the resemblance to Keith Gregg, in his round gray eyes and curly hair.

"Uh-huh." His mouth twitched.

"I am sorry about your dad, Emmett."

"That's okay," Emmett said, as he studied the menu, trying to sound nonchalant. "I'm not."

His face seemed empty of emotion, almost bored. When a couple of high schoolers at the round table hooted at a joke, he gave them a look of disdain—the look a college freshman gives a high school senior only a year younger but *so* much less mature.

"What can I get you this morning?"

He looked at the menu board. "I'll have a regular latte and a cinnamon roll. My mom says they're good here."

"Great choice." I pulled a nice, warm cinnamon roll out of the case with tongs and put it on a plate for him. "I know it's loud and crowded right now, but the high schoolers leave for school in about five minutes. You should be able to find a quiet spot when they leave."

He looked surprised.

"Thanks. Yes, they're *very* noisy." He clutched his plate and latte awkwardly for a few minutes until the students cleared out. Then he hurried to a spot near the window by himself.

Beck came over to me and whispered. "That's Emmett, the councilman's son. I recognize him. I feel so bad for him."

I raised my eyebrows and kept my voice low. "He's not sad that his father's dead. He just told me that."

"My dad used to say there was something off about the councilman," Beck said, as she put a bottle of vanilla Torani away on the syrup rack. "He didn't trust him."

"He might have been on to something, Beck."

When the older crowd had settled in with their drinks, I went to the back room. Maeve was shaping loaves.

I checked my phone. I'd left messages with a few of the local oven owners to see how satisfied they were with their purchase.

I had a text from a baker in Watsonville.

> Hi, Gracie. We love our oven. Totally worth the money. It took us a while to figure out the settings, but now we're able to get more done. No issues and we've had it for a year.

That was good news.
I saw another text – from Nate:

> Just got back in town. Practice tonight.
> Dinner after?

> Let's! 7 p.m. My house.

I went up to the front and saw Emmett gulping down his latte and looking vaguely out the window. He was angry with his dad, I could see that. Could he have killed him in his anger? His mother told me he'd said: *Don't worry, I've got your back, mom.*

I did my not-so-clever ruse of tidying up the napkins, stirrers, and milks at the station near his table.

He'd devoured his cinnamon roll.

"I can take your plate, Emmett."

He handed it to me.

"How's UC Santa Cruz? Your first year's almost over."

"It's okay. I stayed in the area, you know, so I could be there for my mom."

"Sounds like you have a good relationship with her."

"Yeah." He rubbed his eyes like he hadn't slept well and took a sip of coffee. "We had to stick together. My father was a horrible person. I hated him. Now that he's gone, all I feel is, uh—relieved."

A full panel of warning lights went off for me. Was Emmett a killer—or just unlucky enough to have a bad person for a dad? Plenty of kids had bad parents and didn't kill them off.

I wondered if he'd gone to the game Friday.

"Did you ever go see his games? Your mom told me he almost went into the minor leagues out of college."

He shook his head. "Sports wasn't my thing. I didn't go to his games when I was growing up." He pulled a textbook out of his backpack. "Now if you'll excuse me, I need to study for my psych test tomorrow."

"Good luck on that." I watched as he turned pages and hunkered down over his book to review, hoping I'd disappear. "Nice to meet you, Emmett."

When the line at the counter tapered off, I went to the back room, and checked my text messages, mostly looking for oven feedback.

I had a text from the chief.

Time to talk today?

I wanted to get Biga out for a walk. I'd see if the chief could meet outside.

Meet outside? Behind City Hall? I need to take Biga out.

Fine. Meet me in 30 mins.

I shaped my brioche loaves, checked in with Beck and Maeve, then went to Biga's pen and snapped on his leash. He was beside himself with excitement, turning around on his leash till it wound around his legs, craning his neck up, as he looked at me in deep gratitude.

We're going outside! I'm free! I'm free!

To get to the back of city hall, without going inside and giving my little dog the opportunity to pee on the potted plants, we had to walk down a side street. Then we turned into the alley that ran behind City Hall, Clip 'n Curl Salon, and Spinnetti's Sparkletown Cleaners.

I saw the chief standing, one leg up on the steps of City Hall's back entrance.

He looked like he should be taking a drag on a cigarette *a la* James Dean—or even savoring a sugary, deep-fried Laughing Loaf beignet. But these days, the chief was a man of very few vices. And he hated it.

"Hi, Gracie. Thanks for coming over. Corinne keeps trying to sell me on this theory about Runty. It's all she talks about."

"She told me yesterday."

The chief rubbed his face. "I'm wondering if we can offer some kind of reward for the return of the costume."

Biga wanted to sniff out things around the steps, so I had to follow him while I talked.

"She might have a point. The councilman disappeared

and was probably killed during the fifth inning. The Runty costume disappeared from the dugout during the fourth inning, when the River Rats were up."

I told him what Phil Wakeman, the dad at the park last night, said—that he'd noticed Runty going into the dugout in the fourth inning. Then no Runty—just Luke Robbins coming back out *sans* costume, to get food at the concession stand.

"Runty's very recognizable," the chief said. "If someone was out there in the field in that costume everyone would notice."

"Yeah, but it was getting dark then." I pictured the area from my walk last night. "The high grass along the fence would have blocked him from anyone in the stadium."

The chief shook his head. "I guess. But the whole theory's crazy. It's more likely some high schooler stole the costume as a prank."

True, River Grove High School students had done some pranks over the years, some of them legendary. The year before we'd relocated to River Grove, students had painted a portrait on the old bank building of the River Grove High Vice Principal, with fangs dripping blood.

"I also talked with Karen Gregg yesterday—she came into the bakery. She was angry at Keith, but she seemed more frustrated that he died before she could get an apology out of him."

The chief nodded. "I agree with that assessment. She was cooperative yesterday and gave us some helpful information."

"Her son, on the other hand. Emmett told me he was relieved that his father was dead. Seems like he saw himself as his mom's protector. He said that's why he wanted to go to a local college."

"Geez, he's just a kid." The chief grimaced and rubbed the back of his neck. "That's something I need to look into. I'll talk with Emmett."

Biga was obviously bored with the conversation. He'd never shown much interest in the chief. He wandered as far as the leash would allow and finally relieved himself on an RG's Pizza box someone had discarded in the alley.

"Biga!" I pulled on his leash, but it was too late.

The chief grunted. "Never did like dogs."

Somehow, I felt like Biga must have known that.

"Thanks for coming over, Gracie. We've had our ups and downs, but you know I always appreciate your help."

I'd just turned to head back down the alley with Biga, when I saw a head of cropped blonde hair duck down behind the dumpster in back of Spinnetti's Sparkletown Cleaners.

Chapter Thirteen

"Did you just see that, Chief?"

"Looked like Marla Sorenson," the chief said with a frown.

I heard a door slam in the building next door.

"I'm sure it was Marla. She was listening to our conversation." The dumpster was close—maybe twelve feet away. And we weren't trying to keep our voices down. "I wonder how long she was there."

"I heard all about her fight with Keith at practice," The chief said. "Everyone on the team brought it up. But Marla's not a suspect. She has an alibi. She was in the dugout talking to Corinne."

"Then why would she try to eavesdrop on our conversation?"

"Maybe she's a snoop, like someone else I know." The chief started to chuckle.

My cheeks started to burn. When he saw the look on my face, his face sobered up, quick.

"Hey, Dave. Remember how you just talked about us

having our ups and downs? You know what causes some of those downs? When you say things like *that*."

The chief sobered. I thought he'd come back with a comment about how I was just a snowflake and couldn't take a joke.

But he didn't.

He frowned and his mouth twisted sideways. "Gracie, you know I didn't mean anything by it. I say things like that to get a rise out of you sometimes." He looked down at the steps. "I shouldn't do that, and I'm sorry."

What?

Sometimes, I saw it, little signs of change over the past two years I'd known him. The chief had been willing to change his behavior if it helped his relationship with his granddaughter. He'd started eating less sweets, which he loved but were causing him health issues. He was now able to admit when he was wrong—at least sometimes.

It was a slow process.

Sort of like standing there watching a redwood tree grow.

Who said some dogs are too old to learn new tricks?

I tried not to smile too much.

"I appreciate that, Chief."

Biga and I walked back to the bakery, my little dog feeling happy that at last we were moving, not engaged in some boring conversation.

The next time Mayor C came into the bakery, I told myself I'd ask about Marla. Since Mayor C had a past with the woman, I wonder if she knew more about the lawsuit and exactly why Keith Gregg had fired Marla.

But I had a bakery to run. And time was ticking down to the renovation.

Things were falling into place with the pop-up. We had our menu now, and I'd ordered ingredients for our special pop-up offerings.

We needed to do more publicity than just putting out samples for customers to try. I wanted to let people know that they'd need to go to The Riverside's greenspace if they wanted Laughing Loaf coffee and baked goods.

And that come July—or more likely August—we'd be serving lunch.

Beck was great at making cute, whimsical drawings and signs which we displayed at the bakery for new menu items or announcements. But I needed a sign that got our message across firmly and with some urgency.

When we got back to the bakery, I called Marcy from River Grove Printing and asked if she could make another sign, for the bakery's front window, a teaser announcing the special menu items that would be available at the pop-up.

"Gracie, I'd love to do this for you. This is one of the most exciting things to happen downtown in years. I should be able to put this together pretty quickly."

One of the most exciting things to happen in River Grove's downtown in years? Really?

This made me laugh. But after a lot of stress and worry, I could see this pop-up would be a game changer—a new step in my business's life. We weren't shutting down and leaving town for two weeks—we were reinventing ourselves, staying open and bringing our town together in a new and fun experience. The pop-up would show off my staff's creativity and help us segue into a new stage of The Laughing Loaf, as a bakery-restaurant.

There was one more thing I needed to get moving on.

I'd gotten a few more customer responses about the oven I was looking at—both positive. I needed to make a decision. I hadn't heard much negative feedback, even after a search of reviews online. The worst things people said were: *It's really expensive. Allow yourself time to program it to do what you want it to do. You'll probably make a few mistakes.*

So after Beck and Maeve left for the day at 5 p.m., I sat down in front of my computer, took a deep breath, and put in an order for the $12,000 oven.

After debating it and researching online obsessively, it felt good to make a decision.

My DAD only had his individual tutoring session with Jeb tonight, so he ate some leftovers and even took Biga for a walk around the block—which helped me focus on whipping up something for dinner for Nate and me.

I was craving a simple, easy dish that my mom had made when I was growing up—tamale pie. It was great for using up stale tortilla chips, and it was sheer comfort food, nothing fancy.

I layered chips, refried beans, corn, and a ground chicken-sour cream-salsa mixture, and topped it with more cheese and salsa. It smelled tantalizing as it baked.

At 7 p.m., Nate showed up at the door, his face tanned from two days of shooting on the coast.

"Sorry, I didn't get a chance to clean up much after practice." Nate bent down and gave me a kiss.

"I'm liking the tan," I said with admiration as I ran my hand along his jaw.

"And this is less attractive." He smirked. He took off his jacket and I saw how bright red his arms were. "I should know better. I forgot how easy it is to get burnt even when it's foggy."

We sat at the dining room table, and I poured wine and laid out sliced sourdough and some butter.

"Practice wasn't bad tonight. I was worried Corinne and the team would be really down after last week. My time in the slough helped me get out of my funk. I really needed it."

He paused to butter and practically inhale a thick slice of sourdough. "But tonight, it felt good to focus on the game again. To get back to playing together."

"I had an interesting conversation with the chief today." I told him about my talk with the chief—and Marla, the eavesdropper.

He took a gulp of wine. "What a shocker, the chief and the mayor don't agree on something. I'm not surprised about Marla. Maybe she worried she's a suspect and wanted to hear what the chief's thinking."

"You could be right. She sure seemed like she didn't want to be caught doing it."

I brought the tamale pie out and set it on a trivet on the dining room table.

"This was something my mom made when I was growing up. It's big-time comfort food. Not my dad's favorite; he used to call it 'tray of slop.'"

Nate's eyes widened as he watched me set down the steaming, cheesy casserole dish. "I'll take a big slice of slop, please."

I sat down across from him, as he dished some up.

"I'm coming to the game Friday night, with Elana. Kirk won't be with us. Elana said our loud cheering embarrassed him, and she said, rather testily, that she would rather go with someone who didn't 'harsh her mellow.'"

Nate snorted and covered his mouth with a napkin. He was trying hard not to laugh. "I might be on Kirk's side in this one."

"I wish last week's game hadn't spoiled everything. I had a lot of fun, before what happened anyway." I took a drink of wine. "I want to see you and the team play."

"The Gopher Trappers are a tough team." Nate worked his way through the tamale pie on his plate like a man who'd just burned a massive amount of calories. "I don't think we're going to win."

"And why are they called the Gopher Trappers?" I asked. "That's a random name."

"Actually it's not random. The gopher trap was invented in Los Gatos."

"You're serious?" I laughed.

"Absolutely true," Nate said, pushing his empty plate away. "The Macabee Gopher Trap, invented by Zephyr Macabee. And the team wears that name proudly."

With a look that read *how do you know these things*, I left the dishes on the table, and we went to sit on the couch. Nate lay back on the couch, and I leaned back on him. I loved feeling the vibrations in his chest as he talked—and laughed.

"You know what I loved about the game last week?" I relaxed into his chest, the safest place I knew. "I loved watching when you and the team were in the field, tossing the ball to each other. Can I ask you something?"

He looked down at me, a corner of his mouth turning up in amusement. "What?"

"How do you catch the ball like that?" I asked. "It's like you know exactly where it's going. You barely move, just open your glove and catch it."

He kissed the top of my head and let out a rumbling

laugh. "It's a mystical Jedi mind trick. I focus my mind on the ball and guide it into my glove with my *powers*."

"Of course, you do," I laughed.

"Now that I've cleared that up." He moved so he could see my face. "Tell me how you solve your 'puzzles,' as you call your cases."

I didn't have to think about it.

"Persistence. I ask a lot of questions. I connect with people who might know something. It's surprising what people will say to someone who'll listen to them. Then I don't stop till I figure out what happened. I can't get my mind to think of anything else. I'm not sure that's a gift in any way."

He hummed and I leaned into him to feel the vibrations. "I see. So what are you thinking about right now?"

"I'm thinking about *you*?" I looked up at him innocently.

"Nice try." He laughed.

"Fine." I gave him a sly smile. "I don't have the answer yet. I've been trying to figure out who had the strongest reason to kill Keith Gregg. And out of that group of people, who had the availability to do it last Friday night."

I told him about each person on my mental list: Emmett Gregg, with his resentment of his father and protectiveness toward his mother. Marla Sorenson, who was fired by Gregg and lost a lawsuit against him; and Karen Gregg, who had 25 years of anger built up against the councilman. And who stood to inherit a fortune when Gregg died.

"Are you still trying to figure out who took the Runty costume?" He asked.

"Yeah—it's possible the murderer took the Runty costume and wore it as a disguise to go after the councilman. But I have nothing to back that up. The chief wants to offer a reward for the costume's return, I think to placate Corinne."

He thought about this. "That might help someone come forward but *only* if it was a high school prank."

No murderer was going to come forward with a costume covered in his or her own DNA.

I suspected Mayor C was out of luck—and the historic Runty costume was no more.

Chapter Fourteen

I drove to The Laughing Loaf in the dark the next morning, Biga in his crate in the back seat, and my mug of pre-coffee in my cupholder.

I felt the chill in the air. Spring sometimes starts to reveal warm, beautiful things—blue skies, sunshine, and early blossoms—then takes them right back.

I wished I'd grabbed my down jacket when I left the house. It would take a while for the back room to warm up this morning.

I ushered Biga up the back steps. I opened the bakery, stepping into a cold room. I felt like opening up the nice, warm proofer and climbing in with the brioche loaves.

I turned the heat on and clicked on the sound system. I took Biga to his pen, where I unsnapped his leash and let him settle in.

He looked up at me with those big round eyes.

You're going to ditch me here as usual, aren't you?

"We'll try to get outside later, Biga. I mean, c'mon, I'm not a monster."

I searched for a pop playlist on my phone, then

connected via Bluetooth to the sound system. The beat got me moving and warmed me up.

Beck came in at 5:30 a.m., with a plate of apple streusel muffins she'd made at home. She looked tired and red-eyed. Apparently, I wasn't the only one to persist and obsess; Beck wanted to tweak the spice blend in her recipe, so she stayed up till midnight playing with the recipe till she got it right.

"It was driving me crazy. I knew I could get a better blend, so I finally added a little bit of grated ginger." She sighed, a look of relief on her face. "I'm satisfied now."

She handed me one and I took a bite. "*Ohhhh*. Yes. This is better." I took another bite. "Just a pop of ginger, not too overwhelming."

While the sound system played a 1980s synthesizer song, Beck got to work on the beignets and French toast sticks, while I pulled trays of scones out of the freezer. Today's two flavors were cherry white chocolate and cranberry orange. I'd layered them and cut them into wedges, and they were ready to bake.

When Maeve came in at 6:15 a.m., Beck made us espresso drinks and we got back to work, singing along to an Irish-Brit Pop playlist.

I loved the sense of camaraderie as we worked together. It kept anxious thoughts of the Keith Gregg murder and our impending renovation at bay.

For the most part. Until Beck cheerfully spoiled it all.

"Do you realize it's only a week till renovation starts?" she called from the stove, where beignets swirled in hot oil.

"Only a week till the pop-up." Maeve called from the industrial mixer, as she mixed country sourdough. "And I can't wait."

Our new oven would be here in a week, too. I was

starting to get a little nervous about this launch into a new era.

I wanted to share the news about the combination oven and talk to my staff about how we'd have to do some testing and prep in order to begin using it for our bakes.

AFTER THE HIGH schoolers came and went, I did some clean-up in the dining area, which we almost always needed after they left.

I came back to the front counter when I saw a line forming.

"Good morning, Jake. What can I get you?"

Jake Daniels, proprietor of Speed Spot Motors, leaned against the counter, inspecting the display case.

"I need some cinnamon rolls for the gang at the shop. And do you have any of those streusel muffins yet? I had a sample yesterday and really liked them."

I smiled. "You'll have to wait till next week. They're a special item for our pop-up, which will start a week from Monday over at the greenspace in front of The Riverside."

"Wait—what?" Then Jake looked over at the window. "Oh, yeah. The sign says you'll be renovating the bakery. Guess I'll be ordering from there next week."

I smiled. I loved pent-up demand.

I love this thing you baked. What? I can't have it now?

Nope!

Then when can I get it?

One of my favorite sales tools.

I bagged up the cinnamon rolls. "Ready for the game tomorrow night?"

Jake nodded soberly as he took the bag from me. "We

had a good practice last night. They'll be doing a memorial for Keith at the game."

"Really?" Nate hadn't mentioned it. "That sounds like a good thing to do. See you at the game, Jake."

I heard what seemed like a swarm of children come in and looked up to see a familiar face. Phil Wakeman, the dad from Grove Park. He wore jeans and what looked like his best t-shirt today, one that read, DUMPSTER FIRE.

"Hi, Phil. You've got everybody with you this morning."

"I'm taking the kids to school before I go into the shop. Brooke's sick this morning, so I thought I'd give the kids a special breakfast. Got any cinnamon rolls?"

"How many you need—five?" I looked at the kids twirling, laughing, and taunting each other in line behind him. Two of them, the towheaded boys with freckles, looked like twins, which would explain why they all looked pretty close in age.

I'd throw in an extra cinnamon roll, to avoid tears if anyone dropped theirs or had it stolen by a sibling. I bagged them up.

"Hey, I meant to get back to you, Gracie. You asked if we saw anybody carrying a box or bag out of the dugout."

I blinked in surprise. I'd almost forgotten I'd asked. "Oh, yeah. I guess I did."

"Ty here says he saw somebody."

Ty, the straggler from the crazy kid baseball game, pushed his way to the front and put his elbows on the counter.

"I saw this guy. I think he was a teenager. He was kinda small, and he had dark, curly hair. He came out of the dugout with a bag. A Trader Joes bag. He was in a real hurry."

My heart pounded. I broke out in a sweat.

I tried to keep my words even and light. "Did you happen to see where he was going?"

He shook his head.

"Just curious. Thanks, Ty." I nodded at Phil and tried to smile normally. "I was just looking for somebody that night." In the event Phil and his kids knew the Greggs, I didn't want anyone to alert them.

As soon as the line of customers died down, I needed to chat with the chief and the mayor.

Chapter Fifteen

When I went in the back room to replenish the cinnamon rolls in the display case, I pulled my phone out of my apron pocket. I texted the chief and Mayor C.

> Witness saw Emmett G leave the dugout Friday night with a bag

I went back up front to fill the case.

The line at the counter hadn't gotten any shorter.

And why was everyone so clueless?

I'd been very clear with what I'd told customers. The pop-up started a week from this coming Monday—and we weren't serving the special items yet.

"I heard you have macarons, Gracie," Annie Morton said excitedly. "Eric and I are going to Paris for Christmas, and I haven't been able to stop thinking about them. Can I have a dozen?"

"So sorry, Annie." I felt my phone buzz in my apron. "We're not serving them till we're in the pop-up, a week from Monday."

"Darn! Well, thanks, Gracie." She stepped over to look at the display case. "Then give me half a dozen of those cranberry orange scones. Those are our favorite flavor." I wrapped them in a pretty, pink box, then rang her up.

After the line died down, I hurried into the back room to check my messages.

First the mayor's text.

> You sure? Come to City Hall when you can.

Then the chief's:

> Trying to track down Emmett now. I need more details.

I wouldn't be able to get across the street, realistically, till the lunch hour. We were busy today. Marcy had come in early that morning to put up her sign about the special items at our pop-up—and apparently it was already pulling people in off the street. I just wish people had bothered to actually *read* it before coming in.

As I served customers, all I could think of was Emmett Gregg and the possibility that he could be the murderer. That he'd stolen the Runty costume and had hunted his dad down in the tall grass beyond the baseball diamond, to finish him off.

I finally remembered what Elana had said at last week's game. *You have to be small to fit that costume.*

So Luke Robbins, little brother of RGHS class clown Sky Robbins, played the role this season.

Emmett was my height. He'd probably fit.

As I pictured my talk with her in The Laughing Loaf on Tuesday, it hit me.

Karen Gregg was shorter than me.

When the lunch lull hit, I took Biga outside for a pee break and quick runaround in the alley. Then I put him back in his pen.

"Sorry, Biga. I can't take you to all my meetings. Beck will keep an eye on you. So please behave yourself."

Biga looked at me as if I'd personally betrayed him, then with one pained, passive-aggressive look, he went to his bed in the corner of the pen and curled up, his eyes still locked on me.

I crossed the street to City Hall and pulled open the bright green door. Peony was at her receptionist desk, painting the nail of her pointer finger with quick strokes of bright pink polish.

Her head shot up when she heard me. "I'm just fixing my nail, okay? I messed it up at practice last night," she said defensively.

"Fine." I shrugged. "I'm not your boss. I'm here to talk to the mayor and the chief. They texted me."

She sighed heavily and punched the chief's number on her phone.

Why did Peony always bring out the worst in me? I wasn't a mean person. I always felt like one after talking to her.

"Peony, just send her back now." I heard the chief's voice, scratchy on the line.

I went down the long hall, lined with offices for River Grove PD, the mayor, and Councilman Gregg. I peered into the councilman's office, which was open. There was a framed motivation poster on the wall, a buff blond guy looking up at a mountain: IMAGINE....THEN EXECUTE.

I continued to the end to the chief's office.

Mayor C was already there, drinking what looked more

like office coffee—or *ugh*, Keith Gregg's gas station coffee-- than real Laughing Loaf coffee. I realized I hadn't seen either of them at their usual time at the bakery this morning.

"Gracie, have a seat." The chief grimaced.

"I'm trying to get a hold of Emmett, but I need to know more about this witness who saw him."

I pulled open a folding chair leaning against the wall that looked like it had seen better days. I took a seat.

"Phil Wakeman's son, Ty," I said. "The Wakemans were sitting right above the dugout in the bleachers."

The chief frowned. "Ty? He's just a kid. What is he, five years old?"

"He's in middle school, Chief. He said he saw someone —he called him a teenager—with curly hair and glasses, carrying a Trader Joe's bag out of the dugout."

Mayor C nodded. "Luke kept the costume in a Trader Joe's bag."

"I talked to Emmett yesterday." The chief shook his head. "He was honest at least. He told me he was glad his father was dead. But he said he didn't do it."

Mayor C bit her lip. She had a serious, pinched look. "Chief, you need to talk to him again. Marla told me this morning she saw Runty walking out in the park that night."

"When? And why didn't she tell me this when I inter- viewed her?" The chief shook his head.

"Marla's scared of you. She thinks you suspect her."

"Well, for crying out loud." The chief slammed a hand down on his desk with the kind of aggressiveness that would probably scare Marla—or anyone. He picked up his phone and punched in a number. "Marla, please. She is? Well, tell her to come over to my office when she's done. I need to ask her something."

I leaned forward in the unstable folding chair, trying to

keep myself from launching into the chief's desk. "What if Emmett took the costume for someone else?" "There's someone else who could have fit into it—Karen Gregg. Emmett is very protective of his mother."

The mayor connected with my eyes. "She'd inherit everything. She and Emmett."

"Looks like I've got a few more interviews today," the chief said, typing some notes into his tablet.

"If you don't mind," I stood up. "I need to get back to the bakery. We're busy."

The chief waved at me. "Go. I've got my hands full. Thanks for the tip, Gracie."

I walked back down the hall and into the lobby, where I caught Peony holding up a hand, admiring her manicure.

"What do you *want*, Gracie?" She put her hand down immediately and looked at me with heavily lidded eyes.

"Peony, can we talk for a minute?"

Right there, I called Peony's tough-girl bluff. She looked a little scared.

"Talk about what?" She asked, suspicious.

"You and I don't always—*usually*—get along, I know that." She blinked at me, looking puzzled. *Yeah, so what's your angle?*

"Last Friday night, after the game was called off, I stopped by the dugout. When I asked about the councilman's fight with Marla Sorenson, you said he wasn't usually like that—*he has other issues*, you said. What did you mean by that?"

Peony glared at me.

All I did was ask you a question.

Then she looked down at her desk. She spoke calmly.

"Keith Gregg stole money. He took it from my desk. Which—yeah, okay—it *should* have been locked. But nobody thought that was something that could happen in sweet, little River Grove, right?" She rolled her eyes. "There's no proof. But I *know* he took it. I was there late that day. He was still in his office. I went to the ladies room to put on some makeup because I had a date that night. Then when I came back to my desk, my bottom drawer looked a little off. Like someone had shoved it in wrong. It wasn't that way when I left. I hate that the jerk ass did this. There's no way I'd risk the town's funds if I knew there was somebody like that in the office."

"I know you wouldn't. I respect that you do your job well."

She turned red. "I hate him for doing that. It made me look careless."

This confirmed what the mayor had suspected.

"Sorry you had to deal with that, Peony."

She hunkered down over her desk, as if her time was up and she needed to get back to work.

"Thanks. I guess it's all part of being a public official."

I nodded and smiled.

"Thanks for telling me, Peony. See you tomorrow night at the game."

Back at the bakery, it was an hour before closing and there was no line at the counter. Customers sat at the dining room tables, working on laptops or reading. I tried to picture an overlay of the tables and configuration of our new dining area design over what was there now. I felt a shiver of excitement.

Beck was in the back room churning beignet dough in the stand mixer. The room smelled of freshly baked sourdough loaves Maeve had just taken out of the oven.

"Anything new on the case?" Beck looked up from the mixer.

I plunked down in my executive chair by my office. "Maybe something. Looks like we know who stole the Runty costume."

"What now?" Maeve looked up from her loaves, confused. "Did Runty the Rat commit a crime?"

"Possibly." I spun my chair around to face my computer and to start going through today's emails and the snail mail in my inbox. "We will find out soon. Hopefully, soon."

"Sam and I would like to go to the game tomorrow night," Beck said after she turned off the mixer. "Can we sit with you and Elana?"

"Of course. We'd love that."

I scrolled through today's emails, looking for delivery notices for ingredients we'd need for the pop-up specials. Beck and Maeve would practice and fine-tune the specials next week, our last chance before day one of the pop-up.

As I scrolled through the notices, I saw one I wasn't expecting.

It was several days earlier than the company had promised.

So I guess if we had to experience our share of delays over the next few months, we could also experience something *earlier* than we expected. Unpredictability was our season of life right now.

Our new oven would be delivered much sooner than I thought. At a time when we'd be busy prepping for our move to the pop-up.

Like, tomorrow.

At 5 p.m., I heard a timid knock on the back door.

Rose Wilkins stood on the back step. She wore a jeans jacket and a long bohemian-style skirt with a *toile* print that looked like a British nobleman's wallpaper. Slung across her chest was a crossbody purse made out of a book cover of *A Wrinkle in Time.*

"Are you ready for me?" She looked in at Maeve and Beck hard at work over the tables with their baking projects.

"Right on time." I smiled. "Come on in. Maeve, Beck, this is Rose Wilkins. She'll be running the cart back and forth between the Laughing Loaf and the pop-up—and pitching in here and over there."

"Hi, Rose," Beck smiled cheerfully from the metal table, where she'd just dumped out a bowl of beignet dough to roll out. "So good to meet you. Welcome to the team!"

"We're glad you're here, Rose." Maeve came over and shook her hand. "We really, really need you."

I waved her in. "I'll show you around the bakery, so you can get an idea of what we bake and what we'll be doing over at the greenspace. These two here are experts in what they do—Beck on pastries and Maeve on bread."

"I feel like I've eaten everything you make here," Rose said excitedly. "I can't wait to see how it gets made."

I ushered her in to the front counter and then the dining area.

"This will all look different after about two months of renovation." I explained the new style and the counter space that would accommodate the lunch ordering and prep. We'd be staying open till 3 p.m. now, to allow more time for lunch. We'd end our workday at 5 p.m.

I showed her photos on my phone of the pop-up, as Reggie and his staff had helped put up, on the greenspace.

"A week from Sunday will be your first day—that Sunday will be a test run over at the greenspace. So you'll be over with us at the pop-up, then go back to get fresh baked goods from the back room, where Maeve will be working. Beck and I will be in the pop-up."

I showed her the menu of what we'd be serving, then I pulled the metal cart out of the supply room. I'd found one sturdy enough to wheel across the bumpy street and down the sidewalk, back and forth. Rose tried it out, pushing it around the back room, trying out turning corners and stopping quickly.

"It's easy to control," she said.

"Beck and Maeve will have the fresh baked goods on the rack, so you'll just load up and bring it back to the greenspace. You may end up pitching in to help either at the pop-up or back here at the bakery, depending on what we need."

"I can do that," she said breathlessly. "I'm willing to do just about anything. I like to learn new things."

"That's great, because you'll be learning a lot." I smiled. "Let me know if you have any questions. You certainly don't have to stay, but if you'd like to, you can watch Beck, Maeve and I do some of the baking and prep."

She brightened. "I can stay for about a half an hour."

"Wonderful, Rose. I look forward to working with you." I went back to my office, while Rose sat down to chat with Beck and Maeve and watch them work.

The next few days would be crazy, between all prepping for our temporary store, learning how to use a new oven, and figuring out who killed our town councilman.

I sat there, catching my breath for a few minutes, before the storm.

I didn't know then how big this storm would get.

Chapter Sixteen

I was sprawled out on the couch that evening with Biga, when my father came in, definitely not wearing his professorial tutoring outfit.

"Remind me why you're all dressed-up, Dad?"

"Tonight's my dinner at the steak house with Mary Jo," my father said, his eyes glowing. "I'm quite excited to see her."

He wore a navy sports jacket with gold buttons over khaki pleated pants. I think he'd bought the outfit in the 1980s, but I'm sure it would turn the heads of the senior ladies in the steak house.

"Mary Jo says thanks for helping with the resume. She got a call back from the theatre and has an interview next week."

"I'm so excited for her!" I sat up on the couch. "That was quick. Tell her I wish her good luck next week."

"I will, dear," he said absently, as he stood in front of the mirror, adjusting the collar of his buttoned-down shirt.

"I'm glad you two are getting together. Remember, talk about your feelings. And ask about *hers.*"

I felt like a parent sending their kid off to the high school dance: *Be careful and make good choices.*

After he left for his date, I decided to make something special for dinner, just for myself. I never did that. Why not treat myself?

Add to that, I hadn't had any lunch today, and I was starving.

I had salmon in the fridge, which I'd planned on making for me and my dad on the weekend. Salmon wasn't his favorite fish anyway, so I decided to give it a quick marinade and cook it for *me* tonight. I made a marinade with some Thai herbs and fish sauce and made rice in the rice cooker. I topped it all with some roasted carrots and asparagus. When I finally sat down on the couch and ate, I breathed in the exotic scent and savored the flavors. It was all delicious.

I turned on the TV and found a television show based on *Lord of the Rings.* I pulled a throw blanket over myself and completely relaxed.

I was about to fall asleep when my phone rang. Who called anymore?

I picked it up before checking the number. I assumed it was Mayor C or the chief, the only people I knew who would call me.

At first, I didn't understand what the caller was saying. The voice sounded distorted. There was a weird electronic effect on it.

"MIND YOUR OWN BUSINESS, OR YOU WILL PAY FOR IT. THIS IS YOUR ONE WARNING."

The creepy voice sent a chill through me. I hung up. When I checked my received calls, I saw only Unnamed Caller.

Had my questions around town scared someone—

someone who didn't want me to investigate the councilman's murder?

From the day I turned in my husband to the FBI, and when I testified against him in Federal court, I'd received many threats. Some of them scared me—like the ones from actual Russian spies. But some of them rolled off my back.

A threat in a phone call like this was creepy, but I thought of callers like this as small-time cowards. This person hid behind a voice changer and an unidentified number. They called to scare me, but picking up a phone was probably the worst thing they were going to do.

I immediately wanted to call Nate, who was home picking photos to submit from his Elkhorn Slough shoot. But it was only 7 p.m. I could hold out till 9, when he texted. He had a deadline and needed to finish his work so he could play in tomorrow night's game.

At 7:15 p.m., Biga scratched at the back door to be let out. I took a deep breath and opened the back door. I usually went out after him, to get fresh air and to chase him so he got exercise.

Tonight, I waited at the door for him to come back in, scanning the weedy backyard for anything moving. The area looked dark, and the full moonlight turned tree branches into swaying shadows. As soon as Biga scampered back in, I shut and locked the door.

I sat on the couch for a while, trying to read a romance novel Elana had lent me. The characters were silly and didn't interest me in the least. I put the book down, feeling nervous, unsettled.

I finally picked up my phone and called.

"Hey, girl! What's going on?" I heard Elana's bright voice on the other end.

"I just got a threatening phone call. It's probably nothing, but it was a little disturbing. Mostly because my dad's out and I'm by myself."

I felt like a twelve-year-old.

I described the call to her.

"Call the chief and let him know," she said, then I heard her talking to Kirk in the background. "You want us to come over? Kirk and me?"

I felt like a big baby. But I immediately answered.

"Yes, please."

"You got it, girl. See you in a few."

I also texted the chief that I'd gotten the call. He called me right back.

"Gracie, tell me about the call." I described the distorted effect and the short message.

"Gracie, they used distortion because it's someone you've talked to. You know that, right?"

"Yeah, I figured. That's also creepy, so there's a big scare factor. My first thought is that he or she's a coward who isn't going to act on their threat."

"But you don't know that. Want me or Brad to come over?"

"I'm fine." I rubbed my eyes. I must have been feeling more relaxed because I started yawning. "Elana and Kirk are on their way."

In ten minutes, I heard Elana and Kirk at the front door. At first, Biga growled, but as soon as I let them in, he jumped up on their legs and licked their hands. When Kirk sat down on the couch, Biga leaped up on his lap and settled in.

Elana was way too perky for how I was feeling, since I'd been up for almost sixteen hours. But I was glad she was there. Glad both of them were there.

Elana turned on the television and we watched a detective show—probably not the best thing to watch—but I drifted in and out of sleep.

When Nate texted at 9 p.m., I heard the ping and told him what had happened.

> Why didn't you call me?

> I'm fine. E and K are here. I was being a big baby

> Not true. I can still come over.

> Much as I'd like that, I need sleep.

> Be careful. Do NOT be that horror movie girl.

> Me? Never

I felt a little guilty about my last text, since I wasn't sure it was true.

My dad came in at what must have been 10 p.m.—euphoric from what sounded like a successful date with Mary Jo. Until he heard about the phone call.

It took some explanation to assure him I was fine, the chief knew about it, and nothing else bad had happened.

When Elana and Kirk left, I hugged them both. I felt safe, loved and very sleepy.

I stumbled to my bed, followed by my little dog.
I didn't even have the energy to get under the covers.

Chapter Seventeen

I rolled out of bed after hitting my snooze button twice. I never did that. I knew I'd be late, but I really needed the sleep.

Last night's call faded from my mind as I faced a new threat—not getting to the bakery to finish my early morning prep on time.

I felt bad doing it, but I left Biga home. When I rushed to get dressed and frantically pull clean aprons out of the dryer, Biga got up, looked at me, then walked, nonchalant, across the hall to my dad's room.

"So that's how it is? *Fine.*"

I pulled on my clothes, found a clean pair of socks that actually matched, and grabbed my purse.

I locked the house, then ran out to my car, an armful of aprons fluttering in the early morning darkness.

I took in a deep breath of the cool morning air. There was a lot going on today, but it would be a good day and the big game in Los Gatos was tonight. I was hoping it would end well, unlike last Friday's.

The oven would be delivered, and of course, I needed to

pull Maeve and Beck aside and actually *tell* them I'd bought a new oven for the bakery and that—surprise—it was coming today.

When Maeve had put a batch of loaves in to bake, and Beck had finished with the first batch of beignets and French toast sticks, I pulled the two of them over to the metal table.

"I've got something to share with you this morning."

Wide-eyed with curiosity, each took a stool and sat down as I continued.

"We're getting a delivery today. A very *big* delivery. I was planning on talking to you next week about this, but it just so happens it's coming early."

Maeve nodded and gave me a knowing look. Beck glanced back and forth between Maeve and I, puzzled but excited.

"We've had to juggle our bakes from day one. We bake a lot of different things here, and we've had to time things just right, so we can get everything baked and ready at the right times."

Maeve had a big smile on her face.

"So I did some research, talked to a few other bakers, and decided to buy us a combination oven—a 'combi'." Beck mouthed *wow*. "We'll be able to do pastries and breads, and it should be faster than our existing oven. And we can do more multi-tasking."

"Whoa! Gracie that sounds great." Maeve started clapping.

"I heard about this oven in one of the classes I took up in San Francisco," Beck said. "This will help us with a lot of different things—maybe some of our lunch items, too."

"We'll keep the existing oven," I said, pulling up a stool. "We'll need some time to program and experiment with breads in the combi, to get the process down. You and I will need to spend some time with that, Maeve. Pastries won't be as complicated."

My bakers would have a lot more to get used to in the next few weeks. A new outdoor venue. A new fellow employee. And the dust and disruptions that would come with renovation.

"The next month will require some patience from all of us. But we'll get through it. And by August at the latest, we should be serving lunch. Judging by the customers coming in, River Grove is excited about this."

Beck and Maeve started bringing up all the comments customers had made about being able to get lunch at The Laughing Loaf.

"All right, you two. We've got ten minutes till the high schoolers descend on us. Let's do this."

I set out the Laughing Loaf Joke of the Day:

Laughing Loaf Joke of the Day
My wife and I laugh about how competitive we are.
But I laugh more.

The students came in, full of the usual energy. A few wore River Rats shirts and caps, a sign that I'd probably see a few of them at the game tonight.

When Sky Robbins came up to order his Cherry Blossom Latte, I asked him.

"Hey, is your brother doing Runty tonight at the game in Los Gatos? I heard the costume was stolen."

"Yeah, Luke's pretty down about it. Mayor C found a new one at a costume store. But it's not quite the same. It doesn't have that ratty, beat-up charm, with chunks of fur missing. He's still wearing it, though."

"You going to the game?"

He shook his head. "I got a couple of college rejections this week. I'm gonna drown my sorrows in pizza and ice cream. Play some video games."

"I'm sorry, Sky. Wherever you end up next year, I have a feeling you're going to be fine."

"I guess." He frowned. "Doesn't feel great right now, though. Especially when all Jeb wants to talk about are his acceptance letters."

"Yep, I understand. Here's your latte. Hang in there, Sky."

At 10 a.m., I got a message that the oven would be delivered within the 11 a.m.-1 p.m. timeframe, which meant I'd probably need to stick around during lunch.

Not long afterward, Janet from Clip and Curl came in for a vanilla latte and cinnamon roll. She'd given herself pink highlights, which made her look like she'd been in a tussle with a cone of cotton candy. I knew from previous dyeings, this meant she was planning a trip to Vegas with her husband soon.

"You going to the game tonight?" She gave me a knowing eye. "I hear Nate the Great's quite the star player now."

The name sounded odd to me, as if she were implying my boyfriend shouldered his way into that position or enjoyed the fame, which couldn't be farther from the truth.

"There are other great players on the team, Janet." I pulled a cinnamon roll out of the case with tongs. "Yes, I'm going. I'm bringing Elana and Beck and Sam with me."

"I'm going with Karen Gregg. She'll be there for Keith's memorial."

This was odd. It didn't seem like something Karen would do.

"She told me she *never* goes to River Rats games."

Janet gave me a sideways look. "What do you mean? Karen was at the game last week. I saw her."

"Are you sure?" I frowned. "Was she sitting with you?"

She waved her hand. "Karen was a few rows down from me in the stands, on the side. I tried to catch up with her when they stopped the game, but then I couldn't find her."

Beck set down Janet's latte on the counter.

I watched as Janet took her drink and food and headed back across the street to her salon.

I'm sure the chief didn't know this. Maybe Karen wasn't on his list of suspects. She was on mine.

I shot him a text.

> Did you know Karen Gregg was at the game last Friday? She disappeared before they stopped the game.

Chapter Eighteen

Throughout the morning, River Grovians came in for coffee and pastries, some wearing River Rats hats and swag. There was a feeling of optimism among those planning to attend.

As Griff Baxter, son of 1986 Chili Cookoff Champion Scotty Baxter, said: "Sure, a guy got killed last week. But we have a winning team now. And we're gonna beat those dang Gopher Trappers."

"I don't know about that. I heard they're really good." I got him his scones from the case and threw in a cinnamon roll. I really liked Scotty, and he loved them so much. "I put in a little treat for your dad. Tell him I said hi."

"Sure thing. See you at the game, Gracie."

It was nearing 1 p.m., the end of the delivery window for our oven. Why did people bother to set these windows if they're not going to deliver within the timeframe?

I couldn't really start anything, so I checked my phone for any shipping updates. Nothing.

I did have a text from the chief.

> Karen told me she didn't go to the game.
> More news—I'll be over at 4 p.m.

I closed the doors at 2 p.m., with no sign of the oven delivery.

I surveyed the display case. It had been a very busy day, and we were out of everything but a few scones. Nice to end the day on a good note—and in the black.

With no sign of the oven, the three of us did our usual prep and clean up, as we turned on music, and did our usual singing as we worked on our specialties. Maeve shaped sourdough loaves for us to bake tomorrow morning and slid them into the industrial fridge. Beck mixed beignets, which were part of the Saturday morning tradition for many River Grovians.

As I passed by the table where Maeve was working, she looked up and smiled.

"Oh, Gracie? I talked to Rafal and asked if I could stay tonight in River Grove, then come back into Napa a little later tomorrow. I'd like to go to the game with you all, if that's okay."

"I'd love for you to come, Maeve." I hugged her and got a dusting of flour in the process. "We'll save a spot for you."

At 3:45 p.m., there was still no sign of the delivery truck. We busied ourselves with wiping tables and counters and tidying the coffee area. I checked my phone. No word from the oven company or the shipper regarding the delivery. I groaned.

"Hey, you two. If I have to step away for a few minutes to talk to the chief, can you supervise the oven delivery in the back room?"

Maeve and Beck looked at each other.

"Of course. I'm not an expert." Maeve shrugged. "But we had a similar oven at Night Rose."

I smiled faintly. "Great, thank you. This shouldn't take too long."

And of course, both things happened at the same time.

The chief knocked on the front door of the bakery at 4 p.m. I let him in, and he sat down at the corner table. Not long afterwards, a large truck pulled into the alley.

We heard the screech of a truck pulling up next to the back door. A heavy tailgate dropped down with a clang.

"You go ahead, Gracie," Maeve said. "Beck and I've got this."

I took my seat across from the chief. He frowned, circles under his eyes.

"Hi, Gracie. I just talked to Corinne. She came back to me with something, and I'd like to hear what you think."

"What is it?" I searched his face for clues.

"She said she had to change her story." He frowned as he tapped the tabletop with his fingers. "This might be a big deal, or it might not."

"What do you mean, she changed her story?" I studied his face for clues.

"Corinne said that night at the game was crazy. She was trying to track down the councilman, who'd walked off. When I interviewed her that night, she told me Marla was in the dugout with her the whole time. Today she told me that Peony pointed out something. Marla had gone to the restroom for about ten to fifteen minutes during that time."

Fifteen minutes was a long bathroom break, especially during a game Marla was supposed to be playing in.

"Did you talk to anyone else about this, Chief?"

"Just Jake Daniels. He said he thought he saw her

heading for the restroom around the fifth inning, but he didn't see when she came back."

"This changes things." I felt the sense of something falling into place.

"I have to talk to Marla," the chief said firmly. "She doesn't like me, but she'll just have to deal with it."

After he left, I went into the back room, and saw the brand new oven, shiny and looking very high tech, standing in the area we'd cleared out next to our existing refurbished oven.

"It's bigger than I imagined from the photos and videos," I said, as I peeled off the piece of tape that held the oven doors closed.

I joined Beck and Maeve as they stood staring at it, as if an alien spaceship had dropped the shiny oven via tractor beam into our baking room.

"We have a lot to learn," Maeve said, as she put her hand on the shiny metal surface and looked at the row of dials.

"I can't wait to make something in it!" Beck said excitedly. "Can we try it next week? I want to try it with our pop-up specials."

"We should have time. If you're both willing to work some overtime, we could test it in the evenings after our prep." I smiled slyly. "I heard a rumor you guys like to do things like that."

It was 4:30 p.m. and the end of a crazy day. I gathered my purse and bag.

"I'll be back here at 5:30, if anyone wants to meet up to drive over to Los Gatos."

"See you then. I want to see those River Rats win big tonight!" Maeve waved a hand in the air.

An Oven Beyond

I walked across the alley, heading for my Subaru.
As I approached it, I noticed it looked weird.
Lower.
Then I saw it.
All four tires were slashed.

Chapter Nineteen

"Thanks, Maeve." I let out a heavy sigh after I slid into the passenger seat of her tiny VW convertible. Sam had just picked Beck up.

I'd called the chief to let him know about my car.

"How could this happen?" Maeve frowned as she backed her convertible up into the alley and headed for the street, to take me home. "Why would somebody slash your tires?"

I told her about the threatening phone call I'd received last night.

"Do you think it was the same person who killed Councilman Gregg?"

"It could be," I said, as we turned onto the highway. "I guess I should be thankful that a threatening call and slashing my tires was all this person did. I'm sure word spread around town that I was looking into Keith Gregg's murder."

When we stopped at my house, Biga raced to meet me as soon as I came in. I scooped him up.

"You missed all the excitement, Biga."

Maeve nodded at my dad. "I'm Maeve Killoran, by the way. From Dublin."

"I can hear it in your voice," my dad said with a smile. "Thank you for helping Gracie out. I'm very concerned. First the phone call, now the car."

I ran into my room to change quickly for the game, while the two continued talking animatedly about the incident.

I ran to the fridge to pull out the snack tray I'd made and the bottle of champagne I'd been chilling. I was preparing, way too optimistically, for a River Rats victory.

"Ready?" And Maeve and I were off, as Biga watched us leave from my father's arms, FOMO in his eyes. "Beck, Sam and Elana will meet us there."

THE LOS GATOS softball field was in a small grassy park, and I was surprised to see the diamond and small bleachers were even less formal than River Grove's. I doubted the Gopher Trappers were prepared for how many River Rats fans would attend the game. Our fans tended to show up in numbers.

We spotted Beck and Sam low down on the bleachers. They'd spread out their items and bags along the bench to save us seats. Elana wasn't here yet.

I was still a little shaken by the slashing, but it felt comforting to be with people I knew tonight.

"Hi, Sam, thanks for saving us seats." I reached down and gave him a hug. Maeve and I settled in next to Beck, who'd brought a cooler with something interesting in it.

"What's inside?" I asked, eyeing the container.

"It's a surprise." She smiled mysteriously then laid a hand protectively over the cooler. "But we've got a whole game to get through. We can't even *think* about eating yet."

"I hope we have a full game," Sam said, leaning forward, his elbows on his knees. "Please, no murders tonight."

The River Rats took to the field to do their pre-game warm-up. Nate stood at first base, and I realized one advantage of the smaller bleachers here was that I was closer to the field and could see him really clearly. When he spotted me, a full-on smile lit up his face, like the sun coming out from behind clouds.

I hadn't told him about my tires yet. I didn't want to worry him.

Jake, on second base, threw a ball to first, and even though his throw was wonky, Nate caught it easily, like it was no big deal.

Elana was walking toward us from the parking lot, her hand shielding her eyes as she looked for us.

"Elana, here!" I waved my arms so she could see us. She waved back. She was carrying an insulated bag and had a blanket thrown over her shoulder.

She made her way up to us, stepping around people who'd already settled in.

She reached our row and plunked down next to me.

"I brought some wine—"

"Of course," I laughed.

"And some cheese and crackers." She took her sunglasses off. "And a really nice goose liver pate I found in a deli near work."

"I brought sourdough, goat cheese, and some olives." I rooted around in the cooler and brought out the bottle. "And champagne. To celebrate our win. Or cheer us up if we lose. You can't feel sad when you're drinking bubbles."

Maeve leaned over to me, a grin on her face. "I have

never been to a softball or baseball game. Is this the type of food that you eat at a game?"

"It isn't at all," Sam said, chuckling. "It's usually hot dogs, popcorn, and soda."

Maeve turned to Elana and me and lowered her voice. "I would much rather have *your* style of food."

The River Rats came in from the field. I saw Mayor C talking and gesturing as they gathered around her. The Gopher Trappers coach was giving a pep talk to his team on the other side. Nearby, a giant gopher led a group of spectators in a cheer. The spectators were lifting their arms, then closing them together, like a trap snapping shut.

Soon, Runty—Luke Robbins, in the shiny new polyester and foam costume the mayor had ordered—walked out in front of the crowd and began sashaying back and forth in front of the stands. Sky was right: the new costume didn't have the charm of the stolen original.

When the cheer started, now I knew what to do. "RUNTY! RUNTY! RUNTY! RUNTY!"

We screamed, clapped and stomped on the bleachers.

Runty ran back and forth, clutching his tail. He put his furry hands to his cheeks then looked down and pawed the ground with his foot, as if overcome by our admiration.

Then he went up to Mayor C, bowed low, and held out his hand to her. With a tug, he brought her out in front of the stands to dance with him. She laughed and went along with it, and the two did some swing dancing while the crowd cheered.

The announcer came on the loudspeaker.

"Welcome to tonight's match between the Los Gatos Gopher Trappers and the River Grove River Rats. We hope you enjoy the game."

A minute or two later, the loudspeaker came back on with a squawk.

"Now everyone please rise for the national anthem."

At that point, we all stood up, as a recording of someone singing the national anthem played. C'mon--a recording, not a live singer? I'd expect more from Los Gatos, which was bigger and had a lot more resources than little River Grove.

"We will now have a moment of silence for a River Rat player who passed away last week during River Grove's season opener against Gilroy. Tonight we have with us Karen Gregg and Emmett Gregg, wife and son of River Grove Councilman Keith Gregg. Let's pause for a moment of silence to remember the councilman."

All went silent as we all stood for a minute. I can never keep my eyes closed during these things. I looked over to see Karen and Emmett Gregg standing near home plate. Karen appeared to be rubbing her eyes. Emmett looked pained. He blotted his nose distractedly with a tissue.

The announcer handed Karen the microphone. "Thank you for honoring Keith tonight. He would have appreciated this." She nodded and sniffed so loudly the mic amplified it. "Thank you, everyone."

What the heck?

Was this the same Karen Gregg I talked to in The Laughing Loaf? The one who'd vented her anger for what her husband had done—and had suspected him of doing illegal things to other people in town? The one who was so angry at her dead husband she could barely speak?

Was she faking it now? Or had she been lying to me during our conversation at The Laughing Loaf?

Lights flashed on a police car in the parking lot to the far right of us. The chief and Deputy Brad Castro were walking across the grassy area to the bleachers.

I nudged Elana and pointed.

"I'm glad they're here." Elana whispered. "I wonder what's going on."

The game started shortly after this. The River Rats were up, with Peony batting first. This close, I could see the fierce look on her face as she stood at the plate. Was she scowling at the Gopher Trappers, or was she still angry at Keith Gregg for stealing the rec funds from her desk?

The first pitch was low and inside. Peony shot a look of disgust at the pitcher and didn't flinch.

The second pitch flew past her, high. Again, she scowled and held her bat up.

When the third pitch came, it was right in the zone. Peony swung and hit a drive into left field. She sped toward first base and landed on it, right before the outfielder threw the ball to the first baseman.

The River Rats side of the bleachers cheered. Beck, Sam, Maeve, Elana, and I all stood up.

Marla Sorenson came over from the practice area and stood at the plate, bat held up and ready. Since I was closer to the action here, I could see her more clearly. Her light blonde hair peeked out from under her cap. As she did a practice swing, I saw a flash of something. A long streak on the underside of her forearm.

She swung at the first pitch. Then she shook her arm out and raised the bat again.

The pitch came and she hit a foul that flew off to the third base side of the diamond.

"The poor woman looks nervous," Maeve said, her eyes on Marla. "Like she can't seem to find her groove."

On the next pitch, she swung at the ball even though it

looked low to me. She was out. Marla walked back to the team bench below us and sat down, her head bowed. Mayor C sat down next to her and put an arm around her shoulder.

Jake came up to bat next. He walked up and raised his bat, waiting for the ball.

The first pitch came so fast, I could hardly follow its path. Jake swung and missed.

On the second pitch, Jake slammed the ball hard. It landed in the back of the outfield not far from the fence. Two Gopher Trappers scrambled for it, but by the time they got it, Peony was on second and Jake was on first.

All of us in the *de facto* River Rats superfan section were standing and cheering. True, this was just the first inning. But we were doing great right from the start. Or maybe the Gopher Trappers were luring us into complacency before they proceeded to shut us down.

Runty, feeling like this was a good time to whip the fans into spirited cheering, came out and led us in "We Will Rock You." The bleachers shook with the stomping.

We had two players on base. We needed them to score.

Nate walked up to the plate and raised the bat. I knew that look in his eye; I'd seen it when he was completely focused on a heron or a gull he wanted to photograph. He honed in as if he were looking through a rifle sight, waiting for the right time then snapping the perfect shot.

The pitch came, and Nate hit the ball up and out—with so much power it sounded like he'd cracked the bat.

The ball flew in a high, long arc, past the back fence, and disappeared into the tall grass.

Jake watched the path of the ball and immediately took off around the diamond, as Peony headed for home. Nate made an easy victory lap around the diamond, while we all screamed wildly.

All of us River Grovians were standing now, chanting: *Nate the Great! Nate the Great!*

All three batters who had come into home did a group hug then returned to the bench, grinning. Mayor C seemed more restrained; she knew there was a lot more game to be played. Anything could happen.

But even the announcer, presumably with the Gopher Trappers, seemed ecstatic.

"And it's three runs for the River Rats! For Roberts, Daniels, and Behrens!"

Another River Rat came up to bat, someone I'd seen at the last game—Tommy Delgado. He was small and wiry, in his early twenties. He worked at Corner Market, which his dad, Frank, owned. After hitting a foul, he struck out. Then a young woman player named Abby Gorman came up, and unfortunately bunted. The pitcher got to it easily and threw it to the first baseman. The River Rats headed for the outfield.

"That was exciting while it lasted," Elana said, as she opened up her cooler and pulled out a chilled chardonnay, from a vineyard in Paso Robles. She opened it and began distributing plastic glasses full of the golden liquid to the group.

Maeve, Beck, and I eagerly took one, while Sam smiled and shook his head that he wasn't interested.

Beck opened up her carrier and passed a container of macarons down the row.

"Beck, these are gorgeous," Elana said, as she picked two out of the container. Everyone took at least one of the pink, purple, and yellow cookies.

Then I passed around my bread, cheese, and olive platter.

I searched the bleachers and surrounding area to try to

find the chief and Brad. I knew they were here, but I hadn't seen the two since they'd walked in from the squad car in the parking lot.

The game continued. The Gopher Trappers easily caught up to our score. Two batters hit home runs, sending everyone on bases home—until they led us 4-3. Nate tagged a runner out who was trying to steal second base.

I wasn't surprised, but I was hoping—maybe with that familiar River Grove rose-colored optimism—that we'd be able to win tonight, though the odds were against us.

The game was exciting, and I was glad I was here. But a few things tonight had been odd.

"Hey, guys—I'm going to take a little walk. I want to check in with the chief." Both Elana and Beck shot me looks of concern.

Elana caught my eye and lowered her voice. "Gracie, somebody's out there. They had no problem slashing your tires tonight. Who knows what they'll do next?"

I smiled. "I'll be with the chief and Brad. No worries."

I made my way down off the bleachers and scanned the crowd for River Grove's finest.

Other than the park restrooms, there wasn't much here to search. I estimated that if Marla had walked to the restroom, it would have taken about five minutes, max.

I circled the stands, walking past groups of people in conversation and some actually focused on the game. A few young adults were sipping what was obviously liquor from a huge pink Stanley Cup water bottle they passed around, pretending it was water. It made me wonder if maybe it was against regulations for Elana and me to bring booze into the park.

I suddenly felt a hand grip my arm. The arm twisted me around and shoved me into the side of the bleachers. I fell heavily against the iron supports of the stand and felt a sharp pain in my side.

I heard footsteps running away.

"What the hell was that?" The group of tipsy adults turned to me, stunned. "Oh, my God! Are you okay?"

The young woman knelt down next to me.

"Are you hurt?"

I shook my head. She helped me up. The group stood around me.

"Just bruised. Did you see who that was?"

"Somebody in a big down jacket," one of the men said, looking in the direction of the parking lot. "And a ski mask. They ran toward the cars."

The woman looked toward the stands. "Whoever it was, they shoved you hard. I thought I saw a couple of policemen walk through here a minute ago. You should report this."

I felt a pain in my side, whichever way I turned. "Which direction were they going?" I asked.

The group pointed to the back of the stands, where a path led to the park restrooms.

"I'll see if I can find them." I stood fully up and winced as pain shot down my side.

"You sure you're okay?" The woman frowned.

"I'm sore but fine. I'm from River Grove, and I know those two cops."

They looked doubtful. They exchanged glances with each other, but they let me go.

My side hurt more than I expected, and then I remembered it was the side where I'd broken a rib, while being slammed into a pillar under the Santa Cruz Wharf back in December.

I continued around the back of the bleachers. Cheers erupted in the stand above me. Then I heard the Runty chant and stomping feet above me. The Gopher Trappers must have gotten an out.

It was starting to get dark, especially among the trees lining the path. Lights in the park had turned on, sharply highlighting the action on the field.

I came to an opening after the bleachers, where I could see the game. The River Rats were in the field. Nate was at first base, preparing for the batter's hit.

"Gracie!" I heard the chief calling to me, as I paused to brace myself against a sharp pain. "What the hell are you doing out here?"

Chapter Twenty

"I was attacked by someone in a ski mask," I said. "An arm grabbed me, twisted me around and shoved me hard into the bleacher supports."

"A man? A woman?" asked Brad, standing behind the chief. "What were they wearing?"

It had happened so fast, I could only rely on what the circle of tipsy adults had told me.

"Down jacket, ski mask. Other than that, I don't know. It happened so fast. It caught me off guard. The people helping me said the person ran toward the parking lot."

"Gracie, first of all—how badly are you hurt?" The chief looked me over, concern in his eyes. "Do you need me to call EMTs?"

I shook my head. "I'm sure it's just bruises. I'm okay."

"Brad, go back to the parking lot and do a search. Whoever it was is probably gone."

"Got it, Chief." Brad trotted back toward the parking lot.

I pulled the chief aside.

"Chief, something's off here. Karen Gregg was up there

during the moment of silence, acting like she's the grieving widow. I talked to her this week, and she was furious at Keith and suspected him of all kinds of things. Emmett looks like he's actually sobbing over his father's death—not doing a happy dance like he was earlier this week. And poor Marla Sorenson is completely off her game tonight. She looks terrified."

The chief shook his head. "I did think it was strange, seeing Karen and Emmett act like that. But grief is a complicated thing. Maybe they were in shock and the loss of Keith is just hitting them now."

I gave him a skeptical look. I knew what I heard from both of them. I also knew a little bit about grief myself. And their reactions tonight didn't seem realistic.

"Also—why is somebody after me, trying to stop me? Like they have to keep me from revealing some big secret. It's not like I *know* any big secret."

"Oh yeah." The chief stopped for a moment. "I talked to Marla about the restroom break. I got nothing." The chief said in a monotone. "She shut down and gave me that deer-in-the-headlights look."

"Can't say I'm surprised."

The chief waved me to follow him. "Gracie, let's go sit down and watch the game. We might as well enjoy it."

It was a good idea. I wanted to see Nate, and I did want to see the River Rats do their best to win. And after today's events, maybe I needed to chill out.

We took a seat on the lowest row of the bleachers, not far from where Mayor C and the players sat.

We watched the Gopher Trappers' batter hit a fly ball, which was caught by Tommy Delgado in the outfield. Two outs now.

The next Trappers batter had hit one of the home runs

in the first inning. Now he hit a drive down the middle of the diamond. Peony moved into place, squatted down, and scooped it up. She threw it to Nate, who tagged the runner out at first base.

The chief and I stood up, yelling like hooligans. The River Rats came in from the field to bat.

The new, shiny Runty came out in front of the bleachers and led us in another round of "We Will Rock You," then ran behind the gopher and did a sassy dance to taunt the Trappers fans. Runty pointed to the Gopher, then raised and closed his arms together in the trapper motion, aimed at his opponent's rear end. In response, the gopher led the Los Gatos fans in a chant as he pointed to Runty: *Who's going down? You going down.*

"This is really fun," I said to the chief.

"I wouldn't trade this for tickets to a SF Giants game."

I smirked at him. "You would in a minute. Come on, Chief."

Brad Castro came back to report that he hadn't seen anyone in the parking lot matching the description. The chief and I went back to where Elana, Sam, Beck, and Maeve were sitting.

This inning, the fourth, went fast. The River Rats scored one hit, when Peony hit into the infield right past the pitcher. She sped to first base before the Trappers could get the ball to the first baseman.

Marla came up to bat. When the pitch came, she swung too fast. A strike. She swung again on the next two pitches, for an out. She slunk back to the bench and sat down.

"She's got the *yips*," Sam said, reaching for a macaron from the container in front of Beck. "I've seen her before and she's way better than this."

"The yips?" Elana asked. "What's that?"

"It's when you're anxious, nervous about your performance." Sam said. "You think too much about it and you mess up."

After Marla, Tommy Delgado came up to the plate. He hit a fly ball, which the Trappers' shortstop easily caught.

Next, Jake Daniels hit two fouls, then swung and missed. Three outs. The score was Trappers 6, River Rats 3.

The Trappers came in from the outfield. Peony, who'd been stranded on first during the inning, slunk back after them, looking dejected.

A cheesy version of "Take Me Out to the Ball Game" played over the loudspeaker as everyone in the stands got up and moved around for a few minutes, for the fifth inning stretch—since softball only has seven innings, not nine, like baseball. Runty mimicked trudging up a hill, then stood in place, hands held high, to get the crowd started on a cheer.

On the bench a few rows below, Mayor C was talking to the team. She waved and gestured excitedly as she gave what looked like a pep talk. A few of the River Rats nodded.

"This is depressing," Elana moaned as she poured herself a half glass of chardonnay. "Put us out of our misery, you damn Gopher Trappers."

"Hey, we're doing better than we did last year against Los Gatos." Sam looked out at the field as the Trappers' first batter stood at the plate warming up. "They're not destroying us. They'll win, but at least it won't be embarrassing."

The chief leaned into me and talked in a low voice. "Brad says he found something in the parking lot. It looks like a list with notes on it. On a notepad from a fitness club. Gracie, your phone number's on it."

"Wonderful." I sighed. "So this is the killer's to do list? 'Item one: Make threatening call to Gracie Markley. Don't forget the voice distortion!'" I continued, "And lucky me, this person actually works out." I changed position as the pain in my side flared up again.

The chief grunted. "I think it's a significant find. We can compare the handwriting. Clues from the list could tell us who this person is."

I hoped they'd learn something from it. I was just easing down into a vat of self-pity when everyone in our section stood up and screamed: "Go Nate! Nate the Great!"

And I'd missed it. Nate had just tagged one of the Trappers' best players out—a man who'd hit two of the team's homers.

"Brilliant, Nate!" Maeve yelled next to me.

The next batter hit a fly, which Jake caught in the outfield. We all stood up again.

A couple of batters later, with a man on first and a woman on second, the Trapper at bat hit a drive that went right past our pitcher. Peony slid in to pick up the ball and throw it to the third baseman to tag the runner out.

The score stayed at Trappers 6, River Rats 3, until a few minutes later, Nate hit it past the fence, sending Jake Daniels and Tommy Delgado, and himself, home to score runs.

We were tied 6 to 6, until the Trappers came to bat at the bottom of the seventh inning. Nate, Jake, and the River Rats outfield kept the Trappers to one run, bringing the score to 7-6.

You can't imagine how much euphoria and celebration this score caused among the River Rats fans.

Maeve hugged me and Beck.

"Oh, my God. We lost! But not by that much!"

"That was amazing! One point down from the Gopher Trappers!" Elana grinned, pouring the last of the chardonnay into our wine glasses. I decided to save the bottle of champagne for a later celebration with Nate.

The River Rats gathered around their coach and toasted her with what looked like Gatorade. I could see Nate down on the field, talking excitedly with Jake Daniels and Peony. Peony lost her tight-faced scowl and was laughing.

Elana, Maeve, Beck, Sam, and I went down to congratulate Mayor C.

"Congratulations, Corinne! That was an amazing game." I hugged her.

"What can I say? We've got an incredible roster this year." She turned to me and whispered. "We did just fine without the councilman."

The more I heard River Grovians talk, the more I realized that Mayor C was the best thing to ever happen to the River Rats.

I wondered why the mayor kept trying to elbow her way into law enforcement, when she seemed to be a natural at coaching softball.

Nate came up behind us, grinning. He held me from behind and poked his head around my neck. He smelled like sweat and old leather, not a bad smell. "Did you enjoy the game?"

I didn't need to tell him right now about the slashed tires. Or the shove from the masked assailant.

"What a game. Elana and I were cheering you all on. And after the wine, it got a little loud on our row."

"Yeah, I could hear it from the field." He nodded, doing his trying-not-to-smile face.

After a post-game rundown with Mayor C, Nate was free to go. He drove me home, where I heated up some left-over tamale pie for us.

We gushed back and forth about tonight's game. Then,

without thinking, I told him about my car, what Brad had found, and about the person who shoved me into the bleachers. The look of joy faded from his face.

"Gracie."

The hoarse tone as he said my name and the look in his eyes made me scramble to make everything okay again.

"But this to-do list could help pinpoint who is doing this—and who killed the councilman. This brings us closer to a solution. We are *so* close. That's why someone is doing these things. They're desperate."

He swallowed and held my hand. I remembered times when he'd gotten quiet like this. I wondered if he'd take off for a few days for another one of his walking-thinking times in the woods. I searched his face for something.

Shouldn't we be celebrating right now?

The River Rats had just *almost* won. The team had worked together well and prevailed against an opponent who'd trounced them regularly for years. This was the moment he and the team had worked for the past three months.

But it wasn't time to bring out the champagne.

He stood up, grabbed his plate, and pushed his chair back in. Then, because he was Nate, he went to the sink, carefully rinsed his plate and glass off, then put them in the dishwasher.

His face looked drawn as he turned to me.

"I should get home, Gracie. I've had a long day and I still have paperwork to finish on the Elkhorn shoot. If you need help with the car tomorrow, let me know."

He pulled his chair out and came around to give me a light kiss on the cheek. He held my arms and looked me in the eyes.

"Do you understand what it's like for me to hear someone's threatened you? This isn't the first time."

Then he pulled away from me. He quietly opened the door and left.

I went to the couch and collapsed face down, in tears.

Biga came out of my dad's study, saw me, and jumped up and settled in at my feet.

Chapter Twenty-One

The next morning, at 5:30 a.m., I left my little dog behind with my dad.

I tested my bike light to make sure it worked, then pulled my sturdy cruiser out of our storage shed to ride it down to The Laughing Loaf. I was thankful that I'd gotten to sleep in at least a little, since it was Saturday, and we opened an hour later.

It had been a long time since I'd ridden my bike. An even longer time since I'd ridden it in the dark. Hopefully, my bike light had enough charge to get me to the bakery.

A faint wind rustled through the trees on either side of Pilgrim Way, as I rode down it to connect with the highway that ran through River Grove's downtown. The rustling was an eerie yet reassuring sound, as if the trees were awake and watching over me, even this early in the morning.

Every few minutes, I'd turn my side the wrong way, and the pain flared up.

If I'd asked Nate, he would have come over and given me a ride to work. But I resisted that. Maybe out of pride. I didn't know what to say to him. The things I got myself involved with scared him. I didn't have an easy answer for that.

After nearly being run off the highway by a plumber's van, I turned my cruiser onto the gravelly alley behind the bakery. I cast a glance at my poor car, which still looked pretty pathetic, even if it had only had its tires slashed.

At 9 a.m., I'd call Jake Daniels at Speed Spot Motors, even if he wasn't officially open on Saturdays, and ask how soon I could get a set of new tires. I could have a few more days of bike commutes.

I unlocked the back door, then pulled my bike up the steps and rolled it inside. Then I locked the door and turned on every single light in the place, back to front.

I searched my phone for music to play over the sound system. But I couldn't bring myself to listen to the usual jumping pop music this morning. I put on a playlist of quiet indie folk.

I stopped in front of the new oven, shiny and massive. It looked very high tech, with its programmable displays, which I thought was funny. I'd left my previous career to start a bakery so I could get away from tech.

Plunging my hands into dough and creating something as ancient as a loaf of bread made me happy in a way that software never had.

I took cinnamon roll dough out and began prepping the filling, a task I could do without thinking. And my mind went through my list of mental notes from last night—little observations and thoughts I'd tucked away, Post-It Notes stuck in a corner of my brain.

A snapshot of the Greggs—mother and son—looking sad during the memorial time, Emmett trying harder than his mother, maybe, to look the part. Then that firm grip on my arm, someone determined to scare or injure me, so I'd stop investigating.

I thought about Marla, sitting dejected on the bench after a series of mess-ups, in which her body let her down. She'd played well for years, but this season she seemed to be falling apart.

Beck would be here in ten minutes.

I took out my phone and texted the chief. It was 6 a.m.

> Don't want to wake you. Hope your notifications are off. 😊

> Stop by LL today? I need to talk.

Beck came in the back door in cheery mode, her basket filled with fresh eggs from her chickens.

"Good morning, Gracie. That game last night! I had so much fun."

She took off her jacket and started to put the eggs away in the fridge.

"That was crazy, wasn't it? I can't believe how well we did. Nate and Peony were amazing." She continued talking as she pulled beignet dough out of the fridge and gathered day-old loaves to slice for French Toast Sticks. "I'm glad Maeve could come with us."

"The River Rats almost pulled it off." I looked up as I rolled up a slab of dough slathered in brown sugar, butter, and cinnamon. "I don't think I've ever seen the mayor so happy."

Beck pulled out a knife from the magnetic holder on the wall and started slicing a brioche loaf. "I know, right? Maybe it seems crazy to cheer at losing, but it was only by one point. Sam thought Los Gatos would destroy us."

She stopped and looked over at me.

"Are you okay, Gracie?"

I nodded. "Someone pushed me into the bleachers last night, so I'm pretty bruised up today. And I had to ride my bike here this morning, since I couldn't use my car."

It was more than that. It was Nate, who couldn't deal with the threats I'd received. I mean, I got it. It scared and hurt him when he felt I was in danger. I didn't know how we could move on from this.

I didn't share this with Beck.

Beck's face fell. "Gracie, I am so sorry. I forgot about your car. Do you want me to call Sam and see if he can help with the tires?"

I shook my head. "That's nice of you to offer. I'm going to call Jake Daniels at 9 and see if he can help me."

I was thankful it was Saturday. It should be a laidback day in the bakery. Families and couples coming in for coffee. People reading books and playing games in the dining area. It was the kind of day I needed after the craziness of the past 24 hours.

And we were in good shape—as prepared as we could be for the start of remodeling in a week. It was a good thing that we'd gotten the oven early; this coming week Maeve and I could take our time learning how to use it for bread. We'd need to experiment with the steam functions and the settings, to figure out what worked best for each bread recipe we were using. Eventually, when we'd need more bread for sandwich making, the oven would allow us to bake more bread, faster.

Before opening, I looked for a joke related to baseball, since the game would be fresh in everyone's mind. I found one that made me laugh, then printed it out and set it in the holder on the counter.

Laughing Loaf Joke of the Day
Did you hear the joke about the pop fly?
Don't worry about it. It's over your head.

When we opened at 8 a.m., our first customers came into the bakery in good moods. Tristan Conway, his wife Kira, and his little boy, Rowan, came into the bakery. Tristan had won the River Grove Chili Cookoff a couple of years ago, and it had catapulted him from outsider to near celebrity status in town.

Curly-headed Rowan was pressing his face against the display case, and at one point, I saw him stick out his tongue and lick the glass.

"Rowan," I leaned over the counter. "What would you like?"

Rowan looked at me, then solemnly pointed at the pile of fresh French toast sticks in the case.

"Is it okay if I give him some?" I asked Kira, who nodded.

"Just a few. He's a picky eater. He'll probably slobber on them and end up eating one or two."

I put together a small pink box and set two French toast sticks in it, along with a small container of syrup.

I leaned over the counter and showed the toddler what I was giving him. His eyes got big, and he reached his hand up. He wanted them *now*.

"Thanks, Gracie," Tristan said as the took the box from me. "He's thrilled."

A few other families with young children came into the bakery, armed with strollers, blankets and board books.

When I got a break, I took out my phone and went into the back room to call Jake Daniels.

"Hey, Jake. I'm wondering if you can help me. Someone

slashed my car tires here last night. What would be the best way to get them fixed?"

I heard Jake whistle on the other end of the line. "Whoa, Gracie. Don't see that around town very often. You know what? Let me take care of it. I should be able to fix them there. I was planning to go into the shop anyway."

"You sure?" I let out a sigh of relief. "Thanks, Jake."

One problem taken care of.

If only my issue with Nate could be fixed that easily.

THE CHIEF and Mayor C came into The Laughing Loaf at 9:30 a.m., and as soon as customers saw the mayor, they clapped. A few people lifted up their coffee mugs in a toast.

"To Coach Corinne!"

"Way to go, Mayor C!"

"River Rats, River Rats! *Goooo*, River Rats!"

It was funny to me that the team hadn't even won last night. Corinne Webster could have easily gotten her own ticker tape parade down River Grove's main drag this morning.

"What can I get you, Corinne?" I asked.

She studied the display case. "Today is special. I'll take one of Beck's apple tarts, with a big dollop of whipped cream—and a large hazelnut latte."

"Got it—and, Chief, I assume you want your egg on sourdough."

The chief smiled. "Thank you, Gracie, but if you're busy I'll wait for it. And plain drip coffee with some cream." He leaned over the counter. "How are you feeling today?"

"Achy, but better." I tried to smile, but my heart wasn't

in it. I pulled a tart from the case and plated it, then went over to the coffee area to get Beck's whipped cream canister.

I topped the tart with the biggest pile of whipped cream that was stable enough for the mayor to carry. Then I dusted it with edible gold stars left over from Valentine's Day orders.

Mayor C received the plate with excitement. She laughed. "Good Lord, that's huge. Thanks, Gracie."

I handed the chief his drip coffee with cream.

"Hey, Chief? Let me know when you've got some time to chat."

He took a sip of his coffee.

"Sure. Come over to City Hall at noon if you can."

It was busy all morning. Most of the indoor tables were filled. The conversation level was loud and congenial, as people talked about the game. The weather was just warm enough so that being outside was comfortable. The outdoor tables in front filled up fast.

I saw many familiar faces that morning. Sky and Luke Robbins came in to get drinks with their dad, who turned out to be a funny guy—probably the source of his kids' goofy sense of humor. Dan Robbins gave me a thumbs up on my joke of the day.

"That's a good one, Gracie," he said with a chuckle. "And timely."

"Hey, Luke," I smiled at Sky's younger brother as I took his order. "Ever thought of being a professional team mascot? You were hilarious last night. I loved the dance you did with Mayor C."

The thirteen-year-old looked at me very seriously. "It doesn't pay well. I'm going to business school."

Sky scowled at this. He looked tired and was acting more like an eighty-year-old than an eighteen-year-old.

"Whyn't you give me a cinnamon roll and a Cherry Orchard Latte. I'm feeling nostalgic, now that I'm an old senior and all. You still make 'em, right?"

"We still have the syrup." I called the order back to Beck, who nodded. "You got it, Sky." I took a cinnamon roll out of the case for him.

"So, I signed up for community college in the fall." He scratched his head. "My counselor, Seth, said I should do it. He said it's not that bad."

"Good advice, Sky. Of course, it's not that bad. You can find something there you're interested in. Then transfer to a four-year school or just get more training. I'm excited for you."

He shrugged and managed a quick smile. "Yeah. Thanks, Gracie."

He was still feeling competitive with his childhood friend, Jeb. The two may have grown up together, but they would have two different paths in life. I could picture Jeb becoming a professor someday, like his new role model, my dad.

And Sky? Maybe he'd become a standup comedian or even a therapist, like Seth, who had helped him deal with a traumatic event a few months ago.

That was fine and as it should be.

But dang, even though they'd been through their ups and downs the past year, I'd really miss having both of them around.

By 11 A.M., things had quieted down, both in the dining area and outside tables. I asked Beck if she was okay with me popping out for a few minutes.

Saturday was a lazy day in River Grove. The most

action going on was the constant flow of beachgoers who avoided traffic on Highway 17 by taking a short cut through our downtown. In the summer, many of them stopped off to spend time at local businesses, like The Laughing Loaf.

Today our main street was strictly a thoroughfare to get to Santa Cruz.

After timing my crossing for a gap in the traffic, I walked across the street, toward City Hall. But instead of going inside to talk to the chief, I went next door.

To Spinnetti's Sparkletown Cleaners.

The original owner, Aldo Spinnetti, had passed away in the 1970s, and none of his children or grandchildren had continued in the business. The only token of his presence was the retro sign hanging over the front door with a gleaming neon star that lit up over his name at night.

Two women now ran the place: Marla Sorenson and Betty Bonacorsi. Betty had invested in the place to save it thirty years ago, then Marla came on to manage it ten years ago.

The front area of the cleaners had two coin-operated washers and dryers, and when ours were out of commission for a few days last year, I brought our laundry across the street and let it run while I worked. The place smelled clean and fresh. It reminded me that people's two most favorite scents are freshly laundered linens and fresh baked bread.

I walked in to see Marla Sorenson hanging plastic wrapped coats on a rack that rotated through the store. She didn't look happy to see me.

That could be because she'd had a bad game last night and was still down about it.

Or it could be something worse.

"Gracie, what can I do for you?"

"Actually I was hoping to talk to you for a few minutes."

The look on her face immediately changed. Her pale blue eyes widened, looking even more agonized than usual, and her fair skin looked slightly green. Her white-blonde hair, wound up in springy curls, reminded me of the main character in Antoine de St. Xupery's children's book, *The Little Prince.*

"Okay. We can talk." Her voice was already very soft and I hadn't noticed it before, but it sounded like she had a slight speech impediment.

When she glanced nervously around the room, I wondered if she was going to make a run for it. But then she invited me to come around the counter into a back room, where neat stacks of folded clothes lined the counters.

"We can sit back here." She set up two folding chairs for us. The air in this area felt very warm, almost oppressive. Marla was wearing a long-sleeved shirt, so she must be feeling it. Unless she was used to the heat after working here for years.

"I wanted to ask you about this past week with the River Rats." Marla sat still as a stone. "You had an argument with Councilman Gregg at practice the week before last." I felt even more of an intruder, prying into this quiet woman's life in the way I usually did when I was pursuing answers in a case. I wondered if I had any business being here.

But I knew I needed to ask. I had a hunch.

"I'd heard that you worked with the councilman several years ago—and that it did not end well. Was it about that?"

Marla kept eye contact with me.

Her eyes filled with tears. And soon she was sobbing, but strangely, she made no noise at all. Then she spoke softly.

"He fired me. So he could hire someone who'd work for

less money. But the fight at softball practice wasn't about that."

"Good for you for taking him to court, Marla." It was impressive that she'd had the nerve to press charges. "I know that's none of my business. But I also know that you've had a hard time talking to the chief. Is that right?"

She hesitated then nodded.

"Can you tell me what you and the councilman argued about at practice?"

I saw a tissue box on the counter, so I grabbed it and passed it to her. It seemed like the right thing to do. I'm not an easy crier, and I admire people who can just let it out like that.

She took a tissue and blotted her eyes. "I was in City Hall two weeks ago, talking with Corinne. I left her office and was on my way to the front door, when I saw the councilman at Peony's desk. He was pulling out a drawer, looking for something. He took out an envelope—"

"The recreation funds," I said.

She nodded. "I told him to put it back. But he put it in his briefcase. He said if I told anyone what he did, he would make sure something bad happened to me."

"You were arguing with him about that."

Marla nodded. "I told him I was going to tell the mayor. I just wanted him to give it back. The rec department needs that money."

"Then at the game, he told me to meet him by the grass behind the ball park. He acted all friendly. He told me he was glad I caught him at City Hall because he'd done a bad thing. Now he'd changed his mind and wanted to give it back. Then he pulled out a hunting knife. He came at me with the knife in his fist—"

She rolled up her sleeve and I saw the long cut on the

back of her forearm—which I'd seen a flash of at the game last night.

"We struggled but I'm pretty strong. I pushed the knife back at him." Her eyes opened wide with a distant look, as she seemed to picture it in her mind. "Then he fell back. And then I realized. He was d-dead."

I took a deep breath. This made so much sense. She'd been seen arguing with the councilman. She'd eavesdropped on the chief's and my conversation that day, probably trying to figure out what we knew about that night.

"You didn't tell anyone else this?" I asked.

"I was going to tell Corinne." Her eyes scrunched up. "But she's been so nice to me. Even though we're not, you know, together anymore. I couldn't do it."

I remembered something Maeve had once said: "The mayor has a heart of gold. She just doesn't want anyone to know about it." I wondered if the mayor had covered for Marla by saying she'd been in the dugout the whole time during last week's game. But I couldn't see her doing that; in some ways Corinne was as rigid as Peony when it came to following the rules.

Keith Gregg had met Marla out behind the fence with the intention of killing her. She had defended herself.

But if Marla killed Keith Gregg in self-defense, who had been threatening me?

Who'd slashed my tires and then shoved me against the bleachers?

It was not Marla Sorenson, but I had to ask.

"Marla, by any chance, did you leave me a threatening phone call? Slash my tires?"

Marla's big blue eyes looked back at me with a look of utter confusion.

"What?" She asked softly.

"Marla, can you leave with me now? To go talk to Corinne?"

A look of fear flashed across her face. Then she spoke softly.

"Yes. I need to."

&a.

MARLA SHUT DOWN THE SHOP, flipping the open sign to closed, and we walked next door to City Hall.

Peony, working on a stack of files, studied us as if trying to figure out on her own why we were here. Then she gave up.

"We need to see the mayor."

"Fine." She raised her eyebrows and went back to the files she was sorting. "Go on back."

In her office, Mayor C studied both of us, until her face settled into a look of understanding. She leaned back in her office chair.

"Okay, you two. Talk to me."

Marla seemed more at ease telling Mayor C her story. She calmly talked about what she'd seen the Councilman do. She looked a little shaken when she got to the parts where he'd threatened her. And she started crying when she described what had happened in the grass at the ball park.

"I know this is hard for you, Marla." The mayor leaned across the desk and spoke quietly. "But you need to tell all of this to the chief. We already suspected part of this—that the councilman was stealing funds."

"Will you go with me to talk to the chief?" Marla said, her voice shaky. Her skin looked almost translucent, and her eyes looked pained.

The mayor nodded. "Dave should be there. Let me

check." She left her office. I heard her and the chief talking. She poked her head in the door and waved us to follow her down the hall.

"Gracie, if you can come with us—great. If not, I'm sure the chief will want to talk to you later."

I had to get back to the bakery. I'd left Beck on her own for forty-five minutes.

I ran back across the street.

I couldn't tell Beck everything, but she seemed to accept it when I said, "it's something big."

She brightened. "Oh, I forgot to tell you, Gracie—Jake Daniels didn't get an answer from you on his text. He's ready to come over and put on your tires."

I knew the chief would grill Marla. Maybe she'd acted in self-defense, but she'd still killed a man. I'm sure there would be questions as to why she'd waited more than a week to confess to it.

As long as he was growing up, I hoped the chief would step up in his ability to listen and show compassion while interviewing Marla.

Jake came over with high schooler Aiden Franzi, who was still working at Speed Spot and happened to be free for a job today. Jake and Aiden brought a jack and tools and started putting new tires on my car.

While they worked, I went to the back room to start on a batch of brioche. While it was churning in the stand mixer, I pulled my phone out of my apron pocket.

> Chief—call me as soon as you're done with Marla. I just had a thought.

Chapter Twenty-Two

While I waited for the chief to get back to me, I mixed up two batches of scones, read my new oven manual, and did a test batch of cherry white chocolate scones in the new oven.

They came out perfectly, with flaky, buttery layers—and they baked a little faster than they would have in our existing oven.

I'd have Jake and Aiden test out these scones for me. I put together a pink pastry box and filled it with the warm scones. Then I brought some bottles of cold water with me.

Outside, Jake's young employee Aiden had just finished replacing the last tire on my car. The smell of new rubber was strong. Jake squatted down next to Aiden. Four pathetic, ragged tires lay in a pile next to my car.

"You should be good now," Jake said, standing up. "Whoever did this made sure you weren't going anywhere."

Aiden lowered the jack and put the tools in a carry-all.

Just last year, I convinced Jake not to press charges against Aiden for breaking into the backlot of Speed Spot Motors and stealing a catalytic converter. I asked a very skeptical Jake Daniels if he'd give Aiden a chance to use his mechanic skills to pay off his debt. Aiden had continued working for Speed Spot and had become like a second son to Jake and his wife Jeanne.

"I'll come in and settle my bill later, but these are for you both." I handed Jake the pink box. "It's been a crazy day, with a little too much going on. Thanks for taking care of this for me."

As I started up the steps to go back into the bakery, I saw in the corner of my eye, someone riding a bike down the alley, toward me.

My heart pounded when I realized who it was.

Nate pulled the bike up at the back steps. He stepped off and leaned his bike against the railing, right next to where my bike was chained.

"Gracie."

My stomach clenched in anticipation. Was this it? Where he said goodbye?

This was where he'd tell me he couldn't deal with the stress of being in a relationship with the girl in the horror movie, the one who foolishly walks right into danger.

I could understand. For all he'd been through, I didn't blame him.

The look on his face wasn't sad. It was firm. Resolute.

"Gracie, I need to talk to you."

I gulped. I couldn't find any words to say.

"I'm sorry for walking away after dinner last night," he said. "Yeah, when someone threatens you, it scares me. But I like you because you want to figure out puzzles. You're driven to find the truth. If you didn't do that, I'd lose that part of you."

"So—you aren't leaving to go away and think in the woods?" I said, my voice shaking a little.

He put his arms around me. "I did my thinking a long time ago. I'm staying. And finally getting some grief counseling."

By the time I came back inside, exhausted and on wobbly legs, it was 1:50 p.m. Almost closing time.

Customers had cleared out, with the exception of the chief, who sat at his usual table, eating his fried egg on sourdough and downing an extra-large drip coffee.

I slid into the seat across from him at the corner table. "How did it go with Marla?"

"She's going to be okay, though I wish she'd found it in herself to tell me sooner. It's pretty clear it was self-defense. Even the medical examiner had told me the positioning of the knife marks was unusual. It's strange that we never found the knife. Marla says she ran from the scene and didn't look back. When we searched the area, we didn't find it."

"I've been thinking about something, Chief." I leaned back in the chair and rubbed my eyes. It had been a long day. "The threat I got, my car, and getting shoved into the bleachers. What if someone didn't know Marla had caused Gregg's death? They suspected someone else had done it. And they wanted to protect that person."

The chief tilted his head. "When you started asking questions, they saw you as a threat."

"Any news about the to-do list Brad found?" Though I had some suspicions as to who'd written it.

"That letterhead from the gym," the chief said, shooting me a significant look. "Fitness Professionals in Los Gatos. You know, Karen Gregg is a personal trainer."

I remembered that arm gripping me by the bleachers, and I still felt an ache in my side. "No wonder she was so strong."

"Do you have some time, Gracie?" There was a trace of a smile on his face. "Up for a visit to the Gregg house?"

"I have to make sure Beck goes home first." I looked over to see my assistant closing the front door, then heading to the back room to do prep. "She's been covering for me most of today, and she's exhausted."

After I let the chief out, I went and hugged Beck. "The councilman's murder is solved. Just don't say anything to anybody yet. I left you in the lurch today, and I'm sorry. If there's anything I can do, so you can go home, please let me know."

"I'm so glad you figured things out!" Beck hugged me back. "Gracie, really, it was no problem at all. Things got slow this afternoon, so I was able to get some of my prep done."

"I tried out the combi with my scones. They came out great. What do you think about having a baking night next week with you, me, and Maeve?"

Beck's eyes lit up. "Oh, gosh. That sounds like so much fun. Let's do it!"

Chapter Twenty-Three

I checked in with my dad, to make sure he and Biga were okay.

The threats could still escalate–since the chief hadn't released any word that Gregg's killer had confessed. My car had taken a hit last night, and I wanted to make sure my father and Biga were safe.

The chief picked me up at the bakery at 4 p.m.

"I was able to contact a judge regarding the case—and that this is a separate but related charge: obstruction of justice. I have a search warrant, which may help us find the knife." He shrugged. "Once we talk to Karen, we may not need it."

We drove up to Oceanview Drive, past Elana and Kirk's house, to the address of the large home the Greggs had owned.

When we got out, I looked out at the stunning view—a gorgeous vista of the coast, unobstructed by trees. All that money pocketed away by the councilman had bought the Greggs some beautiful things.

Karen Gregg answered the door. The look on her face when the chief showed his search warrant was priceless.

"You'll find nothing here," she said defiantly, though obviously flustered. "Because there is nothing to find."

"Karen, is there a place where we can sit and talk?" The chief asked calmly.

This completely threw her. Her face looked blotchy, her expression puzzled. "I suppose. Come into the living room."

"Karen, we need to inform you that someone has confessed to the murder of your husband. It was an act of self-defense."

She stared at the chief, her mouth open wide.

"What? But he—my Emmett—"

"Emmett didn't kill your husband," the chief said.

Karen Gregg fell back against the door and burst into tears. "It wasn't Emmett. Oh, God, it wasn't him. I was so sure."

While she sobbed, Emmett came into the room.

"I wanted to go out there in that creepy costume and give him the scare of his life. He deserved that. I wanted to kill him, too. But I couldn't."

The chief listened quietly to the young man, a sympathetic look in his eyes. Then he told Karen Gregg that if she had the knife and anything else from the murder site, she needed to bring it out now.

Emmett stared at her. "Mom, what did you do?"

She sat there looking at us, sniffling, as if she were thinking through her options.

Finally, she left the room and brought back a Trader Joe's bag.

The chief and I looked inside and found a hunting knife, dried blood still on it. And a grey, matted costume with a tail and ears.

"I saw you take the costume from the dugout, Emmett. All I could think was that you killed him." She leaned back against the couch cushion, her eyes revealing both pain and relief. "Gracie, I thought you'd figured it all out. It was obvious you were investigating the case, with all your nosy questions for me and for Emmett in The Laughing Loaf. You understand, I *had* to make sure Emmett wasn't arrested. It would ruin his future."

I looked at the mother and her son. Karen Gregg had taken helicopter parenting to a new level.

The chief left it up to me as to whether I wanted to press charges for the tire slashing and the assault.

I told him I'd drop the charges if Karen Gregg paid for my new tires. And the co-pay for an emergency room checkup for my ribs.

The next day, she came into the bakery and wrote me a check.

Chapter Twenty-Four

After a week of hard work, testing the new recipes and tweaking settings on our new oven, it was Sunday afternoon.

Our test run. Tomorrow morning was the debut of The Laughing Loaf pop-up site.

And the beginning of the noisy, dusty demolition phase of our bakery renovation. I dreaded the mess and uncertainty.

Sometimes the only way you can go forward is to walk through a mess.

Maeve had come back early to be here with us for a run-through of what we'd do tomorrow morning. Rose Wilkins was here to practice with the transport cart and some duties in the back room and at the pop-up. She was dressed in full thrift-shop mode--a crocheted top, a patchwork skirt and combat boots.

Reggie's staff and I had set up the tent in the morning, and I'd driven over with the display case. Once the goods were ready, Beck drove over with baked goods to start the day. We'd communicate via text or phone to Maeve and

Rose when coffee was low in the cambros, or when we were low on a particular baked good or milk.

It went okay that afternoon. We served baked goods and coffee from 1 p.m. to 3 p.m. to River Grovians we'd invited personally and those who were just passing by and wanted to check the pop-up out.

When it turned out that our seating area wasn't quite big enough, people solved the problem themselves by sitting on the grass. Families who showed up laid out blankets. Toddlers practiced walking on the grass. A young woman and her friends played ukuleles in a huddle as they drank their coffee and ate macarons. In the distance, a couple tossed a frisbee.

"Best workplace ever." Maeve had come over to the pop-up to join us. She took a bite of the focaccia she'd made, now displayed in all its beauty on a tray next to our display case. "And we get to do this for two weeks."

"Probably for longer," I cautioned. "Realistically there will be construction delays."

"But is that really a problem now?" Maeve smiled as she wrapped a sourdough loaf in a Laughing Loaf bread bag and handed it to a customer. "Would it be so bad if we had the pop-up for longer? Everyone's so happy out here."

The chief and Mayor C walked up to the pop-up.

"Coffee please," the chief asked. "I know you can't cook eggs out here."

"We can't," Beck said. "But how about peanut butter on sourdough?"

Beck grabbed a knife and spread peanut butter on a slice of sourdough. She handed it to him on a paper plate.

"That's being resourceful," the chief said, grabbing the plate and his cup of coffee. "I'm fine with this."

The mayor opted for an apple streusel muffin with her

coffee. "Thanks, Gracie. You know, after our win this past Friday night, we're now tied with the Gopher Trappers in the league standings."

"Nate told me," I said, after I sent a quick text to Rose that we were low on coffee. "Congratulations, Corinne. I can't wait till the next game."

"I don't know if you heard," the mayor leaned toward me. "Marla's back to her old self. She's batting just fine now."

When we neared the end of our Sunday pop-up test, my phone buzzed. I pulled it out of my apron to check. It was Nate.

> Sunset's at 7 tonight. New heron nests on the coast! Up for a bird walk?

I thought of all I'd have to do tomorrow—and the noise and dust that would fill The Laughing Loaf starting at 8 a.m.

I knew there was nothing more I'd rather do this evening than walk along the beautiful coastline, stalking herons with my bird nerd boyfriend.

I started bagging leftovers from the display case, as I watched families on the greenspace pick up their blankets and herd their children together. Maeve and Beck had just boxed up paper plates and cups, napkins, and plastic ware. Maeve lifted the box and the two headed for my car parked nearby, giggling about something they planned to do during the week.

I looked up from wiping down the table to see two familiar faces. I blinked because I couldn't place them at first. So much had changed since my father and I had seen them last. Uneasiness stirred in my stomach.

Federal agent Jeremy LaValle, dressed in his usual River

Grove attire of a beer t-shirt and jeans, took off his sunglasses.

His partner, federal agent Maura Piccelli stood behind him in a pink gingham sundress. As usual, she was subtly monitoring the surrounding area for threats, noting who was close by.

"Gracie, we've received some news," she said in a low voice. "It's imperative that we talk to you about it. Now."

Thank you

Thank you for reading *An Oven Beyond!*
If you enjoyed this book, please consider leaving a review or
rating on Amazon, Goodreads, or the book review site of
your choice.
I truly value the time you take to do this, and it makes my
author heart happy.

Also by Victoria Kazarian

COZY MYSTERY

Drop Dead Bread - Laughing Loaf Bakery Mystery #1

Bread to Rights - Laughing Loaf Bakery Mystery #2

Trouble You Don't Knead - Laughing Loaf Bakery Mystery #3

Sourdough & Cyanide - Laughing Loaf Bakery Mystery #4

Proof of Death - Laughing Loaf Bakery Mystery #5

Stop, Drop and Rolls: A Laughing Loaf Bakery Short Mystery
(prequel novella)

TRADITIONAL MYSTERY

writing as VL Kazarian

(Detectives Ruiz, Grasso and Flores):

Swift Horses Racing – Silicon Valley Murder Book 1

Across the Red Sky – Silicon Valley Murder Book 2

A Tree of Poison – Silicon Valley Murder Book 3

About Victoria Kazarian

Victoria Kazarian lives and writes in San Jose, California. After working for years as a Silicon Valley marketing professional, she taught high school English and actually owned a bread bakery of her own called The Laughing Loaf. When she's not writing, she enjoys baking artisan breads and forcing her children and dog to go on road trips to the Pacific Northwest. See what she's up to at victoriakazarian.com

You can contact Victoria—or perhaps leave a message for Gracie Markley herself—at TheLaughingLoaf@gmail.com

Acknowledgments

This book was a lot of fun to write.

Thank you to my editor and idea person, Honest Magpie, aka Armen, for the editing and developmental help. And to my beta readers—Kerry Nozicka, Faye Friesen Meyers, and Pamela Milliken—for catching things like mysteriously re-appearing dogs, confusing dialog attributions, and awkward batting stances. Special honors to beta reader Chris Anderson for spotting those pesky timeline issues that I completely miss.

As always, I'm so grateful to Mary Ann Askins for her eagle eye proofing and cheerful encouragement.

Thank you, UC San Diego Softball's own Deena Pederson for answering my softball questions. Go, Tritons!

I continue to be grateful for Sisters in Crime Coastal Cruisers' write-ins, where we encourage each other, solve the world's problems and often actually write.

Thank you to my husband, Pete, for your support and for being okay with getting takeout so often.

Finally, thank you, dear readers, for your excitement and support for this series.

Are you in a book club?

Interested in reading any of The Laughing Loaf Bakery Mysteries with your book club? I'd love to appear at your book club online - and possibly in person, if you're in the San Francisco Bay Area.

Contact me at thelaughingloaf@gmail.com

Laughing Loaf Bakery Recipes

Maeve's Focaccia
Apple Streusel Muffins
Gracie's Mom's Tamale Pie

Maeve's Focaccia

Time to completion: 3 hours

A delicious bread, baked in a 9" x 13" pan, that goes great with pasta dishes or can be used for sandwich bread.

1-3/4 cups warm water
2 teaspoons granulated sugar
1 tablespoon dry yeast
4 cups of flour
2 teaspoons sea salt
3/4 cup extra virgin olive oil, also keep the olive oil bottle nearby for coating your hands
Coarse or flaky sea salt for topping
Chopped rosemary or veggies for topping

This works best in a stand mixer that has a dough hook. But you can also mix it and knead it yourself in a large bowl.

Start by mixing the warm water and sugar, then sprinkling the yeast on top of that. Make sure the yeast bubbles/gets foamy.

Add the yeast/water mixture to the flour and salt and

mix till a shaggy dough forms. Continue mixing in stand mixer—or by stirring and kneading the dough—for about five minutes or until sticky and well blended.

Brush a large bowl with about two tablespoons of the olive oil. Scrape out all of the dough from the mixer or mixing bowl and put it in this large oiled bowl. Cover with plastic wrap and let rise for 1 to 1-1/2 hours or until it's doubled in size.

Bring out a 9x13-inch baking dish and coat the insides with olive oil. Now rub olive oil on your hands. Take the ball of risen dough, then put it in the oiled pan, pressing the dough out to the edges. Cover with plastic wrap and set in a warm place to rise again—about 45 minutes or until doubled. Halfway through this time, preheat your oven to 425 degrees.

Once it's risen, take off the plastic cover.

Press your fingers in to make indentations across the dough (I usually do 4 pokes by 6 or 7 pokes).

Sprinkle the dough with sea salt and chopped rosemary. If you want to get creative, you can cut pieces out of red, green, and yellow peppers and use some dill or rosemary sprigs to make representations of flowers or plants. It looks cool! You can look up some designs online to give you ideas.

Bake at 425 degrees for 20-30 minutes or until golden brown.

Apple Streusel Muffins

Time to completion: About an hour

These are moist, comforting and, with the streusel topping, a little decadent. Pour yourself a cup of coffee and sit down and enjoy one for breakfast. Or dessert.

For the muffins:

2 cups all purpose flour

3/4 cup brown sugar

2 teaspoons baking powder

2 teaspoons ground cinnamon

1/2 teaspoon ground ginger

1/2 teaspoon non-iodized salt

1/2 cup canola oil

1/2 cup buttermilk

2 large eggs, beaten

1-1/2 teaspoons vanilla

1-1/2 cups peeled chopped Granny Smith apples

Streusel topping:

1-1/4 cups all purpose flour

1/2 cup brown sugar
1/3 cup granulated sugar
1/2 teaspoon cinnamon
1/4 teaspoon non-iodized salt
6 tablespoons butter, melted

Preheat oven to 375 degrees.

Lightly grease (or spray with oil spray) a 12-count muffin tin. You can use muffin/cupcake liners if you prefer.

In large mixing bowl, mix flour, brown sugar, baking powder, salt, cinnamon, cloves and ginger.

In separate bowl, mix your wet ingredients: oil, buttermilk, eggs, and vanilla till blended.

Now add the wet ingredients to the dry, blending them but not overbeating them. Add the chopped apples and stir till combined. If you overbeat the batter, it can result in dry muffins.

Divide batter into the 12 portions in the muffin tin. Set this aside, while you prepare the star of the show—the streusel topping.

Streusel topping

Mix the flour, sugars, cinnamon and salt together till blended. Then pour the melted butter over this, mixing it with a fork until the mixture is moistened, and it forms lumps around 1/4-1/2 inch diameter. Don't overmix. Then carefully spoon this mixture over the top of the muffins. Then bake on the middle rack of the oven for about 22-24 minutes, or until you can insert a knife and it comes out clean.

Let these muffins sit for about 10 minutes, then remove them carefully from the muffin tin by circling a knife around each and lifting them out.

Enjoy! They probably won't last long, but you can store these in a sealed plastic container, which will keep them fresh and moist for 2-3 days

Gracie's Mom's Tamale Pie

Time to completion: 45 minutes

This is comfort food, nothing fancy at all. It's easy to put together and is a great way to use leftover tortilla chips.

Ingredients

    1/2 - 3/4 bag of tortilla chips
    1 pound of ground meat (chicken, turkey, pork, or beef)
    2 teaspoons tomato paste
    2 teaspoons garlic powder - or 2 cloves of minced garlic
    1/2 teaspoon cumin
    1/2 teaspoon salt
    3/4 cup frozen corn kernels
    1/2 cup red salsa
    1/2 cup sour cream
    1/2 - 3/4 cup milk
    1-1/2 cup grated cheddar or Monterey Jack cheese
    1 can of smooth restaurant style refried beans

You can use regular refried beans, but it helps to break it up and mix it with 1/4 cup salsa to make it spreadable.

Spray a 9 x 9 inch square pan with cooking spray, then line it with tortilla chips.

Cook the ground meat till fully done, then drain. Then mix in tomato paste, garlic, cumin, salt, corn, salsa till the mixture is heated - then stir in sour cream and milk till the mixture is sloppy. The sloppiness will saturate your chips and make them tamale-like. If you need a few more tablespoons of milk to achieve the sloppiness, go for it!

Now pour this mixture into the chip-lined pan. Spread out evenly.

Now layer more chips over the top of this and spread about 1/2 of the grated cheese over the top.

Layer refried beans over that, spreading out to the sides of the pan.

Now crunch up about a dozen chips and sprinkle them over the refried beans, then sprinkle the rest of the cheese evenly over the top.

Bake at 400 degrees for about 25 minutes, or until the cheese starts bubbling up the sides of the pan.

Alternative: You can also add an extra layer of rice, on top of the meat mixture, then continue with the chip layer, and then complete the remaining layers described above.

Enjoy!

Follow me!

If you're on Facebook, follow me at **Victoria Kazarian - author** for additional recipes and content I'll be posting about *The Laughing Loaf Bakery Mysteries.*

An Oven Beyond Playlist

To sing along with the songs Gracie, Beck and Maeve sing as they bake, listen to the *An Oven Beyond* playlist on Spotify.

An Oven Beyond playlist